Built Of Second Chances

A MIDNIGHT SECURITY ROMANTIC SUSPENSE NOVEL

SMALL TOWN HEROES ROMANCE
BOOK FOUR

JEMI FRASER

Just Jemi Books

ISBN 9798223036647

Turtle icon by Freepik on Flaticon.com

Cover design by JB and Jemi Fraser

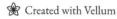 Created with Vellum

To everyone who has earned a second chance
And to those still working on it

CHAPTER 1

In Plain Sight

P addling a canoe while ice formed along the shoreline of the lake was a definite first for Tessa Flores. She'd never experienced anything like this back in Texas.

That thought had her shoving the paddle in too deep and almost swamping the canoe. She'd long ago trained her brain never to think of her childhood or her home state. Why had her thoughts gone there?

It certainly wasn't the tranquility surrounding her. This kind of relaxation hadn't been a part of her life when she'd been a kid. In this quiet haven east of Vermont's mountains, she didn't have to worry about asking the wrong question or seeing the wrong person.

She shoved the memories away then closed her eyes and recited the facts to the quiet forest around her.

Tess Flores.

Born and raised on a farm southwest of Salina, Kansas.

Parents Robert and Gloria had died when she was nineteen, when a tornado had destroyed the area.

She'd graduated with a zoology degree from the University of Wyoming.

She'd lived in six states since, always looking for the perfect job.

1

Now she lived in Vermont, collating data on native species of fauna and flora.

Tessa opened her eyes and rubbed her hands together to warm them up. Her life depended on those facts. She had no business thinking of anything else.

She returned her attention to her fish finder. Well, turtle finder. Her friend Tansy Cheveyo, who owned the property, had helped her modify the tool to search through the sludge at the bottom of the lake.

This was Tessa's first test day and she wanted to collect a baseline of data. With a stroke of the paddle, she pushed past the memories and into the present. She focused on the icy feel of the soft breeze on her face. The warmth of her scarf and mittens. The call of an owl. What kinds of owls wintered in Vermont?

So many new things to know. So many possibilities to explore. She hoped to spend the year learning the area in all its seasons, collecting data that would guide her future investigations.

Once she arrived at her first potential turtle site, Tessa picked up her improvised measuring pole and lowered it carefully so as not to cause waves. When she felt the resistance of the mud, she opened the voice recorder on her phone and recorded the data. Then she lowered the pole again. As soon as she touched something hard, she stopped. She didn't want to disturb the turtle's slumber stage or put it at risk.

She'd found her first turtle. Excitement at the discovery had her grinning. After she'd brought up the tool, she did a careful shimmy in the canoe. Of course, she couldn't be positive that had been a turtle, but it could be. At the very least, she had the depth of the mud layer. Her first experiment in Vermont was a success. Well, it would be.

Smiling, Tessa picked up her tablet and opened the app she'd created. She enlarged the map and confirmed her location on Midnight Lake as best she could. Then she added a data point and input her depth measurements for both the turtle and the mud layer. The thrill she got at the first input of firm data might make her a nerd but she was a happy nerd.

She'd be able to compare the depth of the layers over the next few years to find out if climate change was affecting the turtles' slumber periods. There would be other measures to collect as well so she could see what factors skewed the data. Ice depth and average temperatures for starters. New weather patterns meant that nature was changing in many ways. Ice that stayed on a lake too long, or not long enough, could create havoc on the surrounding biome.

The data she collected would help her figure out solutions. It might not be the career she'd dreamed of when she was a kid, but it was a good one. She was using her skill with numbers and patterns to help the animals and the planet. She could almost pretend it was her passion. At least the FBI consultations she did fed her love of numbers and data.

It took three hours to get to the other end of the lake. There were a lot of turtles preparing to spend their winters slumbering at the bottom of Midnight Lake. She hoped to follow the turtles over the following summer and figure out which species slumbered where. That would improve the data. So far, she'd identified at least seven different turtle species on the lake. It would be interesting to compare them.

Tessa pulled the canoe up to the dock in front of the cabin farthest from Midnight Lodge. It was like being alone in the universe and she loved the setting.

She wasn't sure she would ever be able to walk the distance from the lodge to the cabin, but whenever she had the canoe out, she stopped here.

It was a tiny cabin with a front deck that had a perfect view of the sunrise. She couldn't see the lodge or any other cabins from the small dock. When she sat there, all the worries, all her fears, disappeared.

Tessa had met Tansy several years before through an FBI consult they'd both worked on. They'd been friends ever since and Tessa treasured their connection.

When Tansy had offered her home to Tessa, it hadn't taken her long to accept. She'd been moving every few years for safety, but she hoped this new home would offer that so she could stay in one place.

Tansy and her brother Joe had inherited the property from their grandfather. A parcel of over thirty acres surrounding Midnight Lake with a huge old fishing lodge that now housed Tansy and her friends. There was even an old sawmill and a blacksmith shop on the property.

In this quiet section of Vermont, there were far more trees and turtles than people. And best of all, the lodge was a two-mile hike in from the road.

Not that her legs appreciated the hike, but the safety it added to her new home was priceless. There was a solar-powered golf cart she could use to cover the distance if she needed.

Maybe she could get Graham Buchanan to convert one of the old snowmobiles to solar power to help her make the trek to this cabin in the winter. The man was a genius with vehicles and electricity. He shared the Midnight Security business with Tansy's fiancé and a few others.

Tessa tied the canoe up at the dock and hauled herself up. A flash of movement on the porch had her smiling. The stray cat wouldn't admit it yet, but she was starting to trust Tessa. The saucer of tuna she'd left out sat empty and the tiny cat had hung around after eating. Waiting for Tessa.

"Come on, Ginger. You can come inside where it's warm. You don't have to be out here on your own." She continued to speak softly as she crept up to the porch. The cat peeked around the wall and watched her, but when Tessa paused, she scampered off again.

Tessa waited a few minutes and kept talking, but the animal didn't reappear. She sighed and unlocked the door with the code from the app on her phone. After a few dangerous incidents on the property over the past few months, Tansy had invented an app that connected to the lock that scrambled the code every day. Every building on the property was equipped with similar locks and they would keep out most people. Of course, a determined person could break in the windows, but Tessa had already peeked through the front window. The only other window was intact and the cabin was secure.

Once inside, Tessa wrapped herself in the blanket that rested on the couch. It was too late in the day to stay long, so she wouldn't fire up the pellet stove, but she wanted to warm up her body before she headed back.

The old injuries had healed as much as they were going to heal and she'd learned to cope with them. She'd also learned enough tricks to help her avoid revealing her weakness to others.

Weakness led to questions. Questions led to lies. And guilt. And then another move.

She didn't want to screw up this place. Didn't want to leave. Was it possible to have a forever home? She hadn't believed in forever in over a decade. She wasn't sure she'd truly believed it even before then.

Although one boy had made her want to believe. No. She couldn't think of him. Couldn't remember him at all. That way lay heartache and danger.

Shaking her head at her stray thoughts, Tessa paced the cabin's room and planned her next steps for data collection. Tomorrow she'd start cataloging the birds who stayed in Vermont for the winter. Her first step would be to find where they roosted and nested.

Instead of thinking about *him*, she'd collect more data and try to capture a stray cat.

She'd focus on the future.

Not the past.

Flynn Walker was glad he'd switched from his cowboy boots to hiking boots and traded his Stetson for a knitted cap. Vermont at the end of November was no joke.

As part of the FBI's organized crime unit, Flynn had spent most of his adult life in big cities in the southern US. Far different from the ranch where he'd grown up on the outskirts of Houston.

He'd worked in Chicago for a month one January and that had been an eye-opener. He'd learned to be prepared. And that layers were the key to not freezing your ass off.

Flynn grabbed his duffel and then climbed out of the rental car and locked up. Early winter at Midnight Lake was going to require another learning curve. One he was eager to take.

He'd leaped at the chance to partner up with some of his buddies when Sam Young wanted to jump the FBI ship and start up a business aimed at training people to protect themselves and others. Even if it meant spending time in actual winter.

Flynn looked around the area where Sam had instructed him to park. A huge old sawmill took up most of the lot, but it was a treed area with paths in different directions. He knew they lead to other buildings, mostly sheds, but one that was an old blacksmith shop.

The parking area behind the sawmill had a half-dozen electric charging stations and another couple that were hydrogen chargers. Something he knew nothing about.

Sam's wife, Tansy, was a scientist and inventor. She'd pulled the entire property off the grid. He'd met the tiny woman a few times and she was a real spitfire. Quiet as a mouse, but always thinking and putting those thoughts into action.

Sam's voice broke into his thoughts. "Well, well, if it isn't the King of the Rodeo gracing us with his presence."

Flynn shot his finger up at Sam even as he walked over to haul his friend into a hug. "Your Tansy figure out how to make it snow to try to scare me off?"

From behind him, Graham's voice chimed in. "If this much snow scares you, you're never going to make it. We're going to have to thicken your blood, cowboy."

A stunning redhead walked with his buddy. They must have been in the sawmill when he drove up.

He shook his friend's hand, then hugged him as well. "Good to see you, Buchanan."

"You too, Flynn. This is Aisling Gallagher. She's mine, so keep your thoughts and hands to yourself."

The woman blushed but laughed. Then she reached forward and pulled Flynn into a hug while Graham growled.

Flynn laughed and hugged her again. "Quite the place y'all got here."

Sam grinned. "It's part yours too. Come on, let's start in. Tansy texted that she's got a pot of minestrone simmering. That'll warm up your bones."

Graham smiled. "He won't need it. He's probably soft from working in the city. The hike in will have him sweating and crying for mercy."

They laughed and talked shit throughout the hike. Two miles

through the bush. Hard to believe people lived like this in a world that was more *go-go-go* than *take your time and stroll*.

Hard to believe he was now one of those people.

"How long are you going to stick around? You have enough vacation time to see you through to the new year?" Sam asked.

Flynn nodded. His boss had basically kicked his ass out of the office because he'd accrued so many vacation days. "I've got six weeks for now."

Sam raised his eyebrows. "You've got more than that banked?"

Flynn nodded again. "I did some undercover work earlier in the year." He'd never do that again. It had nearly sucked his soul dry.

The two men nodded and Aisling frowned at him. "Graham tells me you're in the organized crime division. I can't even imagine how difficult it is to work undercover with those types of people."

Graham took Aisling's hand and kissed it. Flynn knew they'd had a tussle with some counterfeiters a few weeks back and that Aisling had been hurt in the process. Thankfully, her injuries hadn't been serious and they'd caught the creeps. But Flynn's job was a reminder of that.

Since chipping in with his friends a few months back to get Midnight Security up and running, he'd been wondering what it would be like to follow in Sam's footsteps.

His buddy had quit the FBI to do this full time. Was Flynn ready for that? His job was demanding and exhausting. And hugely satisfying. He thought this one would be the same.

Lots to consider.

That decision would wait until he took down the Pavic family. He couldn't move on until he'd taken care of that mess and discovered the truth surrounding the death of his friend. Then he'd consider other options.

When they broke into the clearing around the lodge, Flynn grinned. The place was like an old-time fairy tale. No wonder they didn't want to leave.

The three-story lodge was big enough to have a dozen bedrooms on each floor. There was a garage and a shed within sight. He knew there were cabins scattered around the lake as well. The biggest cabin, off to the right, was the headquarters for their security business.

Three dogs broke into the clearing from the right, with Tansy jogging along behind them. She grinned as she approached the group. "Flynn. You made it. Welcome to your home."

Her wording threw him off for a stride but he leaned down to hug her. "Thanks, Tansy." His voice was rougher than usual, but it couldn't be helped.

His home.

The ranch would always be his family home, but he'd never felt like any other place would be a good fit. Maybe this would be his place. It was filled with great people and even greater purpose.

The sun had started to set while they'd hiked in and the scene was gorgeous. Something inside Flynn settled and yearned at the same time.

This might be exactly the right place.

The others headed into the lodge while Sam stood beside him, looking at the lake. Sam slapped him on the shoulder. "It's getting to you. I can tell. This place sucks you in. You may be moving in full-time before you know it."

"Not until I can wrap up the Pavic case."

"Still working that one?"

Flynn nodded. "Always will. I'm not convinced Martin Blanco is dead. I think he killed his daughter in a cover up to go into hiding with the Pavic crew, but I can't prove it."

"What's holding up the investigation?"

Flynn snorted out a laugh. "Almost everything. The Pavic family is slick but small. There are always bigger priorities. They've hidden money in more places than any crime family I know. It's incredibly complex with shell corporations and money laundering around every corner we turn. It's impossible to dig through the data to the core. There's so much with so many twists. We've had teams on the financials, but they can't find the proof we need."

Sam nodded. "It's hard to get through the layers. I wonder if Tess might be able to help."

"Who's Tess?"

"A friend of Tansy's. She moved in a few weeks back. She's a zoologist but a whiz with numbers and patterns. A few weeks ago, she helped

Bella and Mitch figure out a serial arsonist and she's contracted out with the FBI before as a data analyst."

"She's here at Midnight Lake?"

Sam nodded. "She is."

"I'll talk with her. See if she's interested in working through some of it with me."

"Leave it for tomorrow. It's getting late and Tansy likes to have everyone gather for a bit in the evening when possible. She'll want you to meet the others so she's probably making sure everyone's there."

Flynn nodded. He'd been waiting for over a decade to find Pavic, another night wasn't going to make any difference.

A canoe appeared in the dusk and Flynn flinched. There was snow on the ground. This was not canoeing weather. Was it another intrusion onto the property? Although there were approximately a million more effective ways to approach. Especially with him and Sam clearly visible on the shore.

When Flynn jerked his chin toward the approaching canoe, Sam chuckled. "Speaking of Tess, here she comes now."

"Does she know it's almost December? And that she's in Vermont, not Texas?"

Sam laughed. "She's studying turtles."

As if that made any sense. Flynn didn't have a clue what turtles did in the winter, but he was pretty sure they weren't freezing their asses off paddling around the lake. This was the woman who was supposed to help him take down a major crime family?

Sam waved and headed down the dock where Flynn assumed she would tie up her canoe. Curious, he followed Sam.

The light was dim but he could tell she was at least bundled up against the cold. Her long dark hair flowed out of the knitted cap, complete with a pompom. She wore a thick jacket and mittens.

She kept her head down while she maneuvered the canoe close to the dock and then smiled up at Sam.

Flynn's heart stuttered in his chest.

That smile.

That face.

His knees wobbled and then she turned toward him.

The smile froze on her face and for a moment, he doubted either of them breathed.

Then fear filled her eyes. Terror. Absolute terror. It was so vivid, Flynn looked over his shoulder to ensure no one had snuck up behind them.

When he turned back, she was using her paddle to shove back off the dock. "Sorry. I forgot..."

And then she paddled quickly, almost swamping the canoe on the turn. Once she was steadied, she poured on the steam and hurried away across the lake, back the way she'd come.

Sam looked between Flynn and the retreating canoe. "What the hell just happened? Why is she afraid of you?"

Flynn couldn't form words yet.

Sam pressed. "Do you know Tess?"

How the hell did he answer that? "She's not Tess."

"What?"

Flynn rubbed his hands over his face and pulled up the image of the face he'd just seen. It was her.

"Flynn, what the hell is going on?"

Flynn didn't have a clue, but he'd just seen Catalina Blanco. Alive. "She's supposed to be dead."

CHAPTER 2

On The Run

Tessa paddled furiously all the way back to the cabin. Her arms ached and her breathing was loud and ragged.

Hurry.

Get away.

Run.

Hide.

She'd hide for now and figure out how to run. How to hide again.

How could he be here? Had he recognized her?

Tessa reached the dock and pulled up alongside it. It took her trembling hands three tries to secure the canoe with the rope.

Between the cold and the fear, it took her more attempts to clamber onto the dock. She was almost on the deck before she noticed Ginger curled up in a ball not far from the door.

Not wanting to scare the cat, Tessa eased up the final stairs. The cat raised its head and looked at her warily, bringing Tessa out of complete panic mode. She kept her voice to a whisper. "It's warm and cozy inside. Do you want to come in?"

Nothing. Was there anything in her bag a cat might eat? She had a mason jar filled with blueberries she'd been snacking on. Did cats eat blueberries? She knew more about the eating habits of wild animals than domesticated ones.

Keeping her movements slow, Tessa eased the bag off her shoulder and took out the jar. The sound of the jar opening had Ginger jerking up and backing away a few steps.

"It's okay, sweetie. I have a treat. Can you eat blueberries?" She knew most animals instinctively avoided foods that were poisonous to them. A lot of mammals ate blueberries, so she was probably safe.

Tessa tossed one blueberry halfway between her and the cat.

It took a few moments, but Ginger crept forward and sniffed the blueberry, then gulped it down.

This time, she placed the blueberry much closer to her. The cat studied her before pouncing at the treat and then bounding back.

Tessa kept the next one on her fingers and held it out. She believed the cat had either been abandoned or had got lost. A truly feral cat wouldn't have kept returning to a place Tessa frequented.

Ginger had lost her trust for humans and Tessa wanted her to get it back. She wanted to keep her safe, especially with winter coming.

But she wouldn't be able to keep her. Because she would have to leave. Her chest ached and tears filled her eyes. Ginger looked from her palm to her face and back again. One step forward.

Tessa's phone beeped, making both her and the cat jump. Tessa dropped the blueberry. The cat pounced for it, then raced off the deck into the night.

With a sigh, Tessa straightened. The task took longer than normal because the cold had seeped into her right along with the fear.

What was she going to do? First, she'd get inside and get warm. Then she would figure it out.

Once inside, Tessa fired up the pellet stove, but didn't light any of the lanterns. This cabin was on the list of buildings to get solar panels, but that wouldn't happen until the following summer.

Her phone beeped again and she reluctantly pulled it out. A text from Sam. *Are you okay? Where are you?*

She wasn't even close to okay, but she wasn't going to say that. *I'm at the cabin. Sorry for taking off like that but I forgot my things. I'll prob-*

ably crash here overnight. Forgetting her things was a white lie but it was the easiest explanation.

Hopefully Flynn hadn't recognized her.

Flynn Walker. Her Flynn.

She hadn't allowed herself to even think of his name in so long, but seeing him had made it impossible to think of anything else.

Like everyone except a tiny number of agents and doctors, he thought she was dead. By the time she'd woken from the coma, over eight months had passed and her death had been established for her safety.

She hadn't had too many regrets of the things she'd lost with the cover story, but losing Flynn had been the most difficult. He'd been her only true friend. And if she'd been head over heels in love with him, that had been her problem.

Flynn had been one of those kids who'd had it all. Charming, fun, kind to everyone. Sexy as hell in his jeans, western shirts, and that cowboy hat. Even in high school, he'd exuded confidence that he could be exactly who he was.

When he'd asked Tessa to help him out in math one day, it had been the best day of her life. No way should the number nerd and the hot guy have become friends. But they had.

She'd even been out to his ranch one glorious day, where she'd met his amazing parents and his brothers. All genuinely nice people. Warm and teasing. It had been far from anything she'd ever experienced.

That day of family had sustained her through hours and hours of recovery from operations and painful physical therapy. She'd imagined growing up there and having his parents as her own.

Flynn's dad, Marty, had told her she was as pretty as a flower. Then he'd spent the day calling her by various flower names instead of her own name. When she'd had to choose a new name, she'd picked *Flores* as a tribute to Marty and that day.

And *Tess* because of a shared English class with Flynn where she'd had to read the part of a contessa. He'd shortened it to Tessa and called her that for days afterward.

To stop herself from being reminded too vividly of Flynn, she'd put

Tess on the documents. That's what people called her, but she always thought of herself as Tessa.

Every single one of her favorite memories revolved around Flynn and his family. She'd had to shove them down so she could become Tess. Seeing him had broken the dam and they flooded through her.

Why was he here at Midnight Lake?

She'd never allowed herself to do an online search for him or his family. What was a rodeo and horse guy doing with Sam? Sam had grown up in California and had been an FBI agent before starting up Midnight Security. What could he and Flynn have in common?

Going by the look on Flynn's face, he hadn't come expecting to find her. The disbelief and shock had been apparent. She hoped he would blame it on the evening dusk and assume he'd imagined her. That would be the best of all possible outcomes.

Even if she wished she'd been able to hug him and find out everything she could, she knew it would be better if she disappeared again.

She considered contacting the US Marshal in charge of her case, but decided she'd wait until the morning. John would tell her to run now, and she didn't want to. She wasn't even sure she physically could with the stiffness of her body.

If Flynn had brushed her appearance off as a figment of his imagination, she had a chance to stay. Hopefully, Flynn was leaving in the morning and she'd never see him again.

But the thought made her heart ache.

Flynn watched Catalina paddle away and didn't have a clue what to do about it.

She might go by the name Tess Flores now, but she'd grown up as Catalina Blanco.

She'd died as Catalina.

Flynn had cried at Cat's funeral.

So many emotions bubbled through him. He wasn't sure what he was feeling.

Shock.

Relief.

Anger.

Betrayal.

Yearning.

Back to anger.

How could she be alive and not have let him know? They'd been friends. Inching towards more. She'd been so different from the other girls at school and the buckle bunnies at the rodeo grounds.

Catalina had been quiet and shy, but friendly. She'd loved numbers and had been more than happy to share her understanding with anyone who was stuck. She'd never been a snob, even though her family had money.

The day he'd taken her out to his family's ranch had been one of his favorite days ever. She'd loved everything about the ranch, from the horses to the dogs to the food to his parents. She'd talked about it with joy in her eyes every day afterward.

Until she'd died.

Except she hadn't.

There was no way that hadn't been her in the canoe. And even if he hadn't recognized her, the fear in her eyes would have alerted him. It had alerted Sam. And his buddy was waiting patiently for an explanation. One he didn't have.

Was she on a secret mission for her grandfather? Maybe he'd needed her ability with numbers and had planned the explosion so he could place her in another position. Was her presence here a danger to Sam and the rest of the team?

Or had Cat run away and hadn't even known about the explosion until after the fact. That didn't explain the police providing positive confirmation of her death. Or why she hadn't contacted him at some point.

Was she in the witness security program? That would explain a few things. But she should have let him know. He was an FBI agent. He knew how to keep a secret.

There were probably other options, but his brain was too busy dealing with the shock to come up with them. "We knew each other when we were teens. We were friends."

Sam nodded. "What happened?"

"I'm not sure now. But I attended her funeral a couple of weeks before Christmas in our senior year."

Sam swore. "What do you think really happened?"

Flynn huffed out a breath. "It has to be something that would explain the fear we saw. She definitely doesn't want to be recognized."

And it made the Pavic case all the more complicated. He'd started investigating because the day Catalina had died had changed everything. He'd gone from a kid dreaming of winning the National Finals Rodeo to taking all the law classes he could find and then applying to the FBI.

As a kid, he'd heard rumors about Cat's grandfather. Her mom's dad, Grigor Pavic, was reported to be a crime boss. His son Karlo worked for him. Flynn suspected Cat's father had joined the crew.

As soon as he'd joined the FBI, Flynn had started building a file and compiling evidence, which had been incredibly hard to find. Grigor Pavic was slick. Kept his business small enough to keep most law enforcement officials off his back. They had bigger fish to fry.

Not Flynn. He'd learned that three bodies had been recovered from Catalina's house after it had been blown to smithereens. Two adult males burned beyond recognition but assumed to be Martin Blanco and his brother-in-law Karlo Pavic. Flynn had always wondered if they'd set the explosion and then gone into hiding with Grigor.

The only positively identified body had belonged to Catalina and Flynn had never questioned that fact. What else had he been wrong about? Had she been in on the deception, or had she not known about the explosion until later? Why was she living under a different name and not teaching math like she'd planned?

Flynn looked at Sam. "I have to talk to her. Do you think she'll run? Does she have an escape plan in place?" He shook his head at his own words. Of course, she would have an escape plan in place. That had to be standard procedure if she was in Wit Sec and it was smart if she was hiding for any other reason. Cat had been the smartest person Flynn had known. She'd have a plan. Probably several.

Sam sighed. "She's not going to run from there. She'll have to return here first."

"I can't take that chance."

Sam frowned. "I don't know Tess that well. She's been here for a couple of weeks but she rarely talks about herself. I know you'd rather keep this quiet, but Tansy knows her better than I do. She'll have a better idea of what Tess might do. You've got a couple of hours at least before she'll be back from that end of the lake. Come on in and meet everyone and have something to eat. Then I'll talk to Tansy."

"We can't tell anyone else."

Sam rolled his eyes dramatically. "Really? I hadn't thought of that."

Flynn managed a chuckle. "You're sure she won't run from there? Is there an access road out that way?"

Sam laughed. "Nothing but trees for miles. She'll come back this way before she tries to leave."

"How can you be so sure?" Cat could easily walk through the bush and sneak around to get her car.

"Not my story to tell, even if I knew it, but I'm sure. You've got a couple of hours to think it through and button down all that anger surging through you."

Probably a good idea. He wanted to rage and demand answers and apologies. He'd do better once he'd settled with the idea that Cat was alive.

And he'd better start thinking of her as Tess.

Once inside, he met Mitch Robinson and Bella Martinez, firefighter and arson investigator respectively. The entire group sat around a gorgeous live-edged dining table Aisling had crafted for the lodge.

When Tansy said they should wait for Tess, Sam covered it smoothly. He said she'd forgotten her stuff at the far cabin, so she was going back for it and would stay overnight. Apparently it was a rustic cabin with few amenities, but it wouldn't be the first time she'd done it.

Flynn tried to shove the anger aside and was mostly able to focus on the others. Over a meal of pasta, vegetables, and bread, he discovered how much his friends had already grown the business.

Midnight Security had clients who wanted to learn everything from better fitness to defensive driving to tracking criminals in the woods to best practices for protecting their own clients. And more.

Aisling patted Graham's arm. "Just wait until you see Midnight

Runway. It's amazing." Graham had bought an abandoned airstrip and was refurbishing it as a driving school and shooting range.

If Flynn dove in and focused on the business, he might forget about Catalina. Tess. Fat chance, but he had to try. "So, how can I help? What do I need to do to get up to speed?"

Graham grinned. "Well, a herd of cattle got lost in the woods, so I hope you brought your horse and your lasso."

Flynn rolled his eyes but couldn't completely contain the grin. "Sure did. I snuck my filly Ginger in my suitcase, so I'm good." Hell, Cat was really on his brain. Ginger wasn't even his own horse. That was the mare she'd ridden that day at his ranch.

For the next hour, he did his best to stay centered on the group and the business. He helped carry dishes into the kitchen where he had his mind nearly blown.

A cylindrical robot moved off its charging station and to the sink, where it scraped the dishes into compost and garbage bins. Then it stacked everything in a dishwasher that could have been from the future. Afterward, it closed the bins and returned to its station.

Tansy grinned up at him. "Pennyworth likes the job far more than I do. We'll have to introduce you to his cousins after you choose a room. Nico almost shot one and we don't want that happening."

Tansy took him on a tour of the lodge and without knowing it, filled him in a little on Cat. Tess. She'd chosen the room closest to the stairs on the second floor. The one with the quickest exit.

Tansy also revealed that Tess was quiet and hard-working, neither of which was surprising. Tansy was the most brilliant person Flynn had ever encountered and her obvious respect for Tess's work made him happy.

Cat had always been smart and kind. Hard-working too. She couldn't have been any more different from her criminal father. Anger simmered again. What had happened? Why hadn't he known?

Flynn chose a room across the hall from Cat. He wanted to keep an eye on her if she ever came back. He had to see her. After dumping his stuff into drawers, Flynn went in search of Sam.

He found him and Tansy on the deck in front of the lodge. They were huddled close together, leaning on the railing and looking out into the night.

He wanted that. The thought kicked into him like a bull's hoof to the chest. He'd never thought much about settling down before, but seeing his buddy so obviously in love and happy about it made Flynn want it too.

He'd once envisioned having that with Catalina. He'd planned to ask her to the Christmas dance and to be his girlfriend, but her house had exploded. And she'd died.

He'd been painting pictures of the future, and she'd left him behind.

Sam turned at the sound of the door closing behind Flynn. "Thought I might see you. I was just letting Tansy in on the situation."

They turned as a unit and Tansy's face was sad. "Tess never talks much about her past. Actually, she rarely talks about herself at all. Now I know why."

"I need to see her. Can you tell me how to get to the cabin?"

Sam and Tansy exchanged a long look, then Tansy turned to him. "I'm not sure yet. Tess is a friend and I won't betray her trust."

Flynn nodded, impressed with her stance even though it frustrated him. "I get that. Tess and I were good friends in high school. I don't want to get into details because if she's in hiding or on the run, it's better if no one knows them. But we were friends. Starting with her helping me in math, ending with her spending a day with my family at the ranch."

He drew in a deep breath. "The day she supposedly died is the day I was going to ask her to a Christmas dance. She was important to me. I wouldn't do anything to hurt her. I want to talk to her. Find some answers."

Tansy studied him for a long moment. "Fine, but I won't let this surprise her. I'll let her make the decision."

Flynn nodded. That was fair.

Tansy patted her pockets, probably looking for her phone. Sam chuckled and shook his head. "Use mine."

Tansy leaned up to kiss him lightly then she headed down the stairs and out to the dock to make the phone call.

Flynn wasn't sure what he'd do if Tessa said no. He didn't think he could leave it as is. Seeing her face had brought him right back to the emotions he'd been feeling as a kid. A longing for more, for a future with Cat. A yearning for a family of his own, a life filled with love and joy. Now, he was more than a little worried he wouldn't be able to rein those emotions back in.

CHAPTER 3
Second Look

Tessa huddled in the blanket and tried to slow the panic. Flynn Walker was coming to see her. She'd agreed because she knew he wasn't the type to let go of a puzzle. One of the reasons helping him take apart the puzzles in math had been such a joy.

The man had more determination in his belt buckle than most had in their entire bodies. How else would he have been high school champ in bareback and bull riding events?

She'd never seen anything like it. Her father would have had fits if he'd known she'd snuck out to the rodeo that day. Martin Blanco's daughter did *not* associate with cowboys.

And there she was, thinking about her original life again. All because of Flynn. Stopping it was like trying to put the genie back in the bottle. It wasn't happening. She might as well let herself think of it all. Then she could retrain her brain once he was gone.

Tessa's heart ached.

For Catalina. For Flynn. For all of them.

She didn't want to see him at all and wanted to see him desperately.

Her phone beeped. *I'm here.* Sam had obviously given him her number. Tessa forced herself up off the couch and to the door, keeping the blanket around her like a shield. It took four deep breaths and a

21

couple of tries before she managed to turn the deadbolt and open the door.

And there he stood.

All sexy cowboy even in a knit cap, thick jacket, and hiking boots. He was taller and broader than he'd been as a teen. His work on the ranch and his rodeo activities had ensured he was muscular even as a kid, but now he had the energy of a leashed panther.

His frown was aimed directly at her and Tessa worked to keep her fear from showing.

"You going to let me in?"

It took her a moment to get her feet to move, but she stepped back and let him enter. When he brushed past her, her breath hitched.

She could run, but he'd catch her before she was down the stairs. There was no way to get in the canoe before him. She'd considered it while he'd been jogging out with Sam, but rejected it. She didn't want to be a coward. Didn't want to run again.

If there was any chance to save her life here, she would have to fight for it. Fight for it with the man who stood in front of her. The boy she'd loved.

She didn't have any internet connection this far from the lodge or she'd have given in to the need to search for information on Flynn. Find his connection to her life here in Midnight Lake.

Drink in her fill of his image. Because it still filled her up.

Flynn moved past her into the room and she followed his movements. Still the same bit of swagger that cowboys got from riding horses when they were toddlers. Or maybe they were just born with it.

His gaze roved the room, took in the pellet stove and the rustic furniture, then turned back to her. No pleasure or happiness in those eyes. Anger though. Lots of anger.

"Are you going to come in as well, or are you thinking of running?"

His voice was harsh. Tessa kept her face steady as she closed the door and wrapped the blanket more tightly around her. He was the one who'd insisted on seeing her, so she decided he could be the one to speak first. She wasn't going to volunteer anything.

Flynn paced around the couch a few times before he turned to her. "Well?"

She ignored his bark and moved to the kettle she'd set on the pellet stove. She'd set up two mugs with Tansy's cinnamon and cardamon tea. After pouring some into both, she picked up her mug and sat on one side of the couch. Her legs didn't like when she stood too long and she didn't want to show any weakness in the face of his anger.

Taking a settling breath, she looked up at him. "How do you know Sam?"

"What? I find you back from the dead after more than ten years and you want to know how I know Sam?"

She knew Flynn would never hurt her, so she ignored his loud voice and angry demeanor. Their accidental meeting had thrown them both way off kilter. And she wasn't dealing with someone she'd thought was dead.

Flynn had been a boy who studied the odds against him. He'd known every stat there was to know about the bulls and horses he might draw in the rodeo. He'd grown up on a ranch where he'd had to solve the puzzles that every rancher faced on a daily basis. Not knowing how things worked drove him nuts. But she couldn't fix that, not even for him.

Flynn paced a few more times then sat on the chair opposite her. "What happened? What happened back then? They said you were dead. They said they'd positively identified the body."

His voice shook and Tessa's eyes filled with tears. Tears she hadn't shed in years. "I can't imagine what you went through. I'm so sorry you had to go through it."

Flynn put his head in his hands and drew in deep breaths. Tessa swallowed hard against the emotions clawing up her throat.

Finally, he looked up, emotions raw on his face. "Are you on the run? Does your grandfather know you're alive? How did you survive? Why did you hide from me? Are you in Wit Sec?"

Tessa frowned at the barrage of questions before the phrasing of his last words sunk in. Most people said Witness Protection not Witness Security and certainly not Wit Sec.

"You can't tell anyone, Flynn. Please. You can't tell anyone." Her own voice broke and Flynn jumped up to pace again.

"I know. If you're in Wit Sec, I know."

He kept pacing and she knew it had to be hard. He was likely thinking of his parents and his brothers. She was asking him to lie by omission so that she could stay in a home she loved. That wasn't fair. If she disappeared again, she could find a new place and he wouldn't have to lie to anyone.

Even if it meant she'd be choosing another new name. She'd refused the plastic surgery option, but if word got out, she might have to go along with it if she wanted to live. And she did.

Maybe she could give Flynn that gift. Seeing the pain she'd inadvertently caused made her wish she'd never come to Midnight Lake. She hadn't done anything wrong, but her family had.

Flynn shouldn't have to pay the price. He shouldn't have to live with knowing where she was. She didn't want to leave, but she knew it was the right thing to do. "I'll leave in the morning. Find a new name and a new place. You can forget you saw me."

Flynn stopped pacing and frowned at her again. "No way in hell."

Flynn knew he was acting like an ass, prowling like a mountain lion scenting his prey. He couldn't grab control of his emotions or his body. Seeing Cat—no, seeing *Tess* alive in all her beauty was such a shock, he wasn't sure he'd ever get over it.

He needed to sit and talk with her. Tell her it was the situation he was angry at, not her. But he *was* angry at her. And now she was offering to disappear into the ether again because of him.

He managed to growl out some words. "You don't need to leave. We'll figure this out. I'm not over the shock yet. Give me a minute."

"I don't want you to live with lying to your family. If I disappear again, you won't have to do that."

Well, that made him feel like an ass. He did a couple more walks around the room, then sat in the chair he'd tried before. He picked up the mug and looked down at it. "I'm doing this all wrong. Everything is churning around like a pissy bull in the chute. Even though I knew it was you, I didn't actually believe it until you opened the cabin door."

He huffed out a breath and managed to look up at her. "I'm glad you're alive."

Her eyes filled instantly with tears and she closed them. She swallowed hard and pressed her lips together for a moment before she spoke, her words soft and shaky. "Thank you."

"Why didn't you tell me? Let me know somehow?"

Those dark eyes flew open again and he saw a flash of incredible pain before she looked down. She sipped her tea before she spoke. "If you know enough to call it Wit Sec, you know the rules."

He did. And he knew the rules were to protect her, to keep her alive. But it still stung. He wanted her feelings for him to have been big enough to risk the rules. And that was as selfish a thought as he'd ever had.

He put down the mug and pushed up to pace around the room. It was a better use of the energy than yelling at her and demanding answers which he knew she shouldn't give him. But he wanted those answers anyway.

After a third lap, he forced his ass back in the chair. "Were you even in the house when it exploded?"

More pain flashed in her eyes but this time she didn't look down. Instead, she maintained eye contact and nodded.

"Hell. There was almost nothing left of the house." And it had been more mansion than regular house. Probably a dozen fancy bedrooms.

The thought of Cat dying in that explosion had haunted him. He wondered if the thought of her surviving it would do the same. "Was your father in the house as well?"

This time the amount of pain visible in her face and eyes had him moving out of the chair to squat at her feet. He knew she and her father had never had a good relationship. She'd been under pressure to always live up to his expectations and to never make mistakes. Martin Blanco had been—was?—a cold and calculating man.

Flynn ran his hand over the blanket Cat, Tess, was using as a cocoon. Or as a shield from him. "Forget I asked."

"I can't think about it, Flynn. I can't go back into those moments. It's too big. I'm afraid if I let it out, I'll never be able to put it back again. I have to be Tessa now. All the time."

Her eyes pleaded with him to understand. He did. But he didn't like it. He wanted answers. He hated not knowing details. How could he solve the problem or the puzzle if he didn't have all the details?

Except there was nothing about the past to solve. All he had to do was deal with it. Could he? Obviously, he could because there was no other choice. But he wouldn't like it.

"Okay. I get it. I do." He patted the blanket then stood up to pace again.

He needed to talk to her. Get to know her as Tess. Get to the point that he could think of her as Tess. That was the only way she'd be safe.

Except for the fact that he'd been working for a decade on a case against the Pavic family. Her mother's family. The family he suspected had enveloped either her father or her uncle, or both, after the dramatic house explosion.

Rosa Pavic had married Martin Blanco and died not long after Catalina had been born. Flynn couldn't remember Cat talking about her family other than her father and uncle. And only then with a shiver of revulsion. Did she know her mother's family was a crime family? Did she know her grandfather led the organization?

According to Tansy, Tess was a whiz with data and patterns. Which didn't surprise him at all. She'd loved numbers and had wanted to teach math at the highest levels.

Wit Sec had probably squashed that dream. People in their care had to learn to change up their patterns in order to stay hidden. If you were a huge fan of takeout sushi, you couldn't order it because it was a way to track you down.

So many changes. He'd known all that in theory, but thinking about it in connection to the woman in front of him was a whole different thing. She'd had to lock down her dreams and habits and develop new ones.

Maybe he could use that to build a rapport back. Gain a little ground after letting his anger show. "So, zoology? How did that happen?"

Tess's smile was small and sad. "It was very different from numbers but still interesting."

"Do you like it?"

She nodded. "I liked the analysis bits from the beginning, but I've learned to enjoy the more hands-on aspects as well."

"Like canoeing in the snow?"

This smile was more genuine. "Like that. It's nice to see where the data comes from, not just use the data someone else has generated."

And that was the perfect segue into how she could help him, but he didn't want to throw that at her yet. He needed her to trust him first. She hadn't trusted him enough before to let him in on her new life. And while his head knew that was smart, his heart hurt.

"Your turn. What is your job? Do you like it?"

Her soft question jolted him again. He'd assumed she knew who he was, that he was coming to Midnight Lake. "I'm an FBI agent."

Tess's eyes widened and her mouth opened but it took a moment before she spoke. "You're Sam's friend from the FBI? You're a partner in Midnight Security?" The fear was back in her voice and in her eyes.

"Yes."

Her entire body slumped and she looked down into her mug. "I guess that settles it. You have all the connections with these people. You'll stay and I'll go."

"We can figure this out. Tess." There was a hesitation before he was able to add her name, but there was another shock to his system.

He'd said it before. He'd called her Tess before. No, he'd called her Tessa. And that had slipped out of her mouth only moments before.

What the hell did that mean?

CHAPTER 4
Deep Dark Secrets

essa watched as the memory hit Flynn.

He stared at her and she couldn't look away. "Tessa. Contessa. From that stupid play we had to read aloud in English Lit. You hated that play, hated having to read aloud."

His words were soft and hesitant, unlike the harsh ones from earlier. "I called you Contessa for ages after that."

Then he'd shortened it to Tessa. And she'd loved it. She felt as if she could be anyone, do anything. If she could leave her family name behind, she could be who she wanted to be.

A niggle of guilt ran through her again. She'd always wondered if that wish had somehow caused the destruction of her home and the deaths of her father and uncle.

"Why did you choose that name? Wait, did you get to choose your name?"

She nodded and shrugged. "It was a good memory."

That made Flynn frown as he thought it through. Finally, he nodded, but the frown didn't disappear. His eyes had softened though. Those deep brown eyes that had always seen her. Not the daughter of the powerful Martin Blanco. Not the quiet girl who tried hard not to be noticed. He'd seen the girl who'd wanted to fit in. The girl who liked numbers more than she liked most anything the other girls liked.

Flynn had brought her out of her shell, at least a little bit. With him, she'd gotten to know more people at the school. She'd even dreamed of going to the Christmas dance with him.

Kissing him.

Maybe a little bit more.

Those dreams had exploded right alongside her house.

"Why Flores?"

That made her smile and she simply raised her eyebrows, wondering if he would figure it out. If the memory of that day was anywhere near as strong as her own memory.

Of course, he'd experienced his wonderful family every day, so it probably hadn't stood out. Flynn's eyebrows shot up at her smile and then furrowed in concentration. He did like solving riddles.

Flynn was calmer and acting more like the boy she remembered. Was there truly a way they could remain in the same place without endangering anyone?

If her father's associates found out she was alive, she wouldn't be the only one they targeted. She couldn't be responsible for them hurting Flynn or any of her new friends.

Strangely, the only thing that had saved her life that day had been the explosion that had nearly killed her. She still wasn't sure who had blown up the house. Or why. But she'd learned that day that her father and uncle were truly horrible people and that they would do anything for their own gain.

Flynn's eyebrows shot up and his grin had everything in Tessa relaxing. This was her Flynn.

"My dad. Was it because of my dad? He called you all different flower names the day you were out at our ranch. Daisy. Rose. Ivy. Lily. And a whole bunch more I don't remember."

She nodded. It was one of her favorite memories. One she'd tried to twist so that it was her own father trying to make her feel special. Of course, that wasn't possible, but a girl could dream.

She'd dreamed of Flynn and his family a lot over the years. Even when she'd tried to drop everything from her past persona, she couldn't drop those.

"Tess Flores. Contessa of the Flowers. I like it." The warmth in his voice filled her up and gave her a little hope.

And then he pursed his lips and grimaced. "So, you didn't forget me? Us?"

She shook her head as she battled back more tears. For years, she hadn't allowed herself to cry. There was nothing she could do to change things and tears wouldn't help. Flynn's appearance had weakened her resolve and the tears wanted to flow. Relief and joy at seeing him. Fear for her future. Regrets. So many regrets.

"I couldn't forget you." Her choice of name had pretty much ensured she'd think of him every day. Even though she tried to never think his name, never visualize his face. None of her efforts had helped. Even if she'd chosen a different name, it wouldn't have helped.

Flynn Walker had been the strength she'd needed to get her through the past decade and more. His confidence that every puzzle could be solved, that every problem had a solution, had helped. He treated life the way she treated math.

There was always a solution.

And there would be one, now. There had to be. She just hoped it was one that didn't break her again. She wasn't sure she was strong enough to take it a second time.

Flynn nodded seriously and then pushed to his feet to look out the window of the cabin. Strength seemed to radiate from him, and she wished she could soak some of it up.

When was the last time she'd felt strong? Had she ever? She would have to dig deep to make sure she was strong enough to ensure Flynn was safe from her family's reach. Her father and her uncle may have been killed, but she thought it was her grandfather who'd always run the show. Whatever that show was. If the government thought she wasn't safe from them, they were powerful. And evil. And she couldn't bring that danger to Flynn or Midnight Lake.

"Did you call the Marshals after seeing me earlier? Did they give you instructions to move out?"

"No. But I can." It wasn't at all what she wanted.

Flynn shrugged but continued to stare out the window. From this angle she couldn't see his reflection. She wondered what he was thinking, but was too afraid to ask.

Realizing the significance of the name she'd chosen had softened him, but she knew he was still hurt and angry and confused. She knew it, because after thirteen years, she was still all of those things herself.

"I didn't tell Sam or Tansy any details, but Sam figured out from my reaction that I knew you from before. They know I think you're on the run or in Wit Sec. They also know how important it is to keep that quiet. They won't say anything."

Fear rippled through her again. More people knew she was in hiding. More people who could give her away without meaning to do that. More people who would have questions she couldn't answer. So many questions.

Tessa brought her legs up on the couch and wrapped her arms around them. Helplessness filled her. In the last few hours, her life had spun out of control for the second time.

This time would be physically easier. She wasn't waking up from an eight-month coma. She wasn't facing multiple surgeries, not counting the ones they'd done during those eight months. This time, Tessa knew she could walk. Knew she had the ability to become someone new.

She had skills she could use to make a new life. But she'd have to give up her Tessa persona. Her career. Her FBI consults. Even her turtles.

"Can you promise me you won't run before I see you again?"

She looked up to see Flynn studying her. The warmth was gone and his expression was carefully neutral. "Why?"

He frowned. "I need some space and I need to think this through. Can you meet me at the dock at seven tomorrow morning?"

She stared back while she went through her choices. In the end, she nodded. It wouldn't be fair to Flynn if she ran before morning. He needed closure. She'd give him that before she left.

Flynn nodded and headed to the door. He opened it and then bent. "It's too cold to leave your cat outside."

Without another word, he put a startled Ginger on the floor, closed the door, and left.

31

F lynn didn't have a trail to follow, but it didn't matter. Sam had explained the layout of the lake and the position of the lodge. As long as he kept the lake on his left, he'd find it. The alone time would do him good.

What the hell was he supposed to do?

Was he supposed to act as if he didn't know her? That would be impossible. Better to make up a story that they'd met before. It was a big enough risk to have Sam and Tansy aware that Tessa was in Wit Sec. Letting in the other four who lived at the lodge was too big a risk.

They needed a story, even if it was only for a few days. He should have stayed at the cabin and hammered out the story with her.

But how was he supposed to stay when he was blistering with anger one moment then filled with tenderness the next? Hell, he'd wanted to scoop her up into his arms and hold her until they figured everything out. Much better to get the hell out and get his head straight. If that was possible.

Catalina Blanco. Alive. At Midnight Lake.

He should be thrilled and celebrating. Why wasn't he? Because some small part of him didn't believe in coincidences.

What were the odds that he would end up at a parcel of land in the middle-of-nowhere Vermont and meet up with his high school friend who was not only supposed to be dead, but was also the reason for his obsession with taking down the Pavic family and the reason he'd joined the FBI? His entire career, hell, his entire adult life, had been focused around the explosion that day.

Everything in him had changed and he'd switched from dreams of being a rodeo star and living out his life on a ranch to joining the FBI to pursue evil. His career was based on a lie.

Cat had never said much about her family, but he'd known she'd been scared to make mistakes. He'd seen more wariness than love when she'd talked about her father. That wariness edged into fear when she'd mentioned her uncle.

Was that all somehow part of a plot?

If he didn't believe their meeting at Midnight Lake was a coincidence, did it mean that they were both being orchestrated somehow by the Pavics? How?

That required a bigger leap of faith than believing in coincidence. Was the truth at one end or the other, or somewhere in between? Did the Pavics know Cat had survived? Did they know she was now Tess? And if they did, did they know where she lived? And did they know Flynn was tracking them?

So many questions. Too many. He needed some answers. And the woman with the skills and the knowledge to help him was back in a tiny cabin with an orange cat.

Until he was convinced there wasn't an underlying plot to discover what he knew about the Pavics, he couldn't share what he was doing with her. The thought of Catalina being forced to become Tess in order to be turned into a mole trying to disrupt the FBI investigation made him ill.

It also made him realize he was inventing conspiracy theories that were more complicated than the programming Tansy had created to build her TeenySaurs. He was making himself nuts.

Flynn walked through the woods at an easy pace. It was at least a mile to the cabin from the lodge. And another two miles to the road.

If anyone wanted to take out Tessa, they'd have a way to go on foot. They'd have to go through the safety measures Sam and his buddies had installed around the property. And they'd have to find her without GPS or Wi-Fi. Not impossible seeing as the cabin was on the lake. They could use a plane like that arms dealer had done when he'd wanted Tansy's tech.

Flynn blew out a breath. He wished he had a horse. Or a bull he could ride. Something to pull his concentration away from Tessa. That way his subconscious could figure out what to do and how he felt. His active brain was nothing but a mass of confusion.

He considered calling Nico Rivera, another partner in the Midnight Security business. Nico was a top profiler in the FBI. He was an expert at figuring out people and their motives. Flynn could really use his help, but he didn't want to risk bringing in another person who knew Tess's original identity.

His phone showed him it was after midnight when he finally walked into the clearing around the lodge. His friends were making a good place here. A place he was already part of financially. A place he wanted to test out. Find out if it could be home.

Instead of heading inside, Flynn sat in one of the chairs on the deck. They'd all been cleared of snow, but it was still chilly. Sleep wasn't going to be possible, so he might as well acclimate himself to Vermont in winter.

A soft woof had him turning to find the German Shepherd watching him quizzically through the door. Flynn crossed over and opened it. "Hey Jetson. You need to come out?"

The dog stepped outside and then moved to sit beside the chair Flynn had taken. Once Flynn sat again, Jetson laid his head on his lap and stared at him.

Flynn chuckled. "Are you an emotional support dog? You want to take a crack at figuring out what I'm supposed to think, what I'm supposed to feel?"

Jetson gave another soft woof and leaned into Flynn as he patted the large head. They sat together while Flynn patted the dog and stared at the lake.

Eventually the door opened again and Flynn wasn't surprised when Sam dropped into the chair beside him. "Figure anything out yet?"

Flynn laughed without a lot of humor. "Not a damn thing."

"Want to talk it out? The parts you can, anyway. You know I won't repeat anything."

He did know that. Sam was probably the steadiest, most reliable person Flynn knew.

They hadn't worked in the same departments, but they'd crossed paths many times over the years. Sam's reputation was unimpeachable. He was the reason Flynn had bought into Midnight Security. There was no one outside his family he trusted more and Flynn couldn't talk to his family about this. "Have I told you why the Pavic case is so important to me?"

Sam nodded. "Yes. Your friend in high school was the girl killed when—" Sam's voice dropped away and Flynn nodded.

"You got it in one. That girl was Tessa. Of course, she wasn't Tessa then. We were told they'd positively identified her body but that the two male bodies were burned beyond identification. I always wondered if her father had disappeared off the scene. I wondered if he'd killed his own daughter and faked his own death to slide into his father-in-law's organization without any backlash from the people he'd been working for."

Sam swore. "That's convoluted. Which means it fits right in with organized crime families."

"Exactly. It never crossed my mind that C—Tessa might still be alive. All this time, I had it backward."

Sam grunted. "Unless you were right and the other two bodies were fakes as well. Does Tess know?"

Flynn sighed. "I didn't get that far. My mind hasn't absorbed this yet and I haven't handled it well."

Sam didn't show any judgement. "It's a hell of a situation. I think you can forgive yourself for needing some time to figure it out."

Flynn leaned back in the chair. "She offered to leave so I don't have to lie to my family. I asked her to promise not to go until we have a chance to talk again in the morning."

"Does she have to leave?"

"I don't know. She said I have more connections here, so it should be my place. If she disappeared, I wouldn't know anything about her new identity. That way I wouldn't feel like I was holding something back from my family."

"So, she'd start all over again."

It was a statement, but Flynn answered it anyway. "Yeah."

They sat quietly while Flynn patted the dog and stared at the lake, looking for answers.

Sam sighed. "How hard would it be to simply accept her as Tess?"

"While trying to put the rest of her family in jail? Maybe a little hard."

That was the understatement of the century.

CHAPTER 5
Second Guessing

Tessa woke from a fitful doze when Ginger yowled in her ear. She sat and stretched while she reached to pet the cat. "You've decided you like me after all? Or are you hungry?"

The cat had raced around the tiny cabin and had hidden in every spot she could find when Flynn had dumped her inside. She'd yowled and spat every time Tessa had approached. There had only been a few blueberries left, but Ginger had eaten each one out of Tessa's hand before skittering away to hide again.

This was the first time the cat had approached her when she hadn't been offering food. Now the cat backed up out of reach and looked at the jar that had held the blueberries.

"Sorry, Ginger. They're all done. And I didn't bring any food for either of us." Because she'd planned on returning to the lodge the night before and being part of the welcome meal for Sam's friend.

Flynn. Of all the people in the world, Flynn was one of the last she'd expected to show up.

She'd never allowed herself to do an online search for any of the people from her past. That was one of the rules for Wit Sec, and she'd followed it. Even private browsers weren't really private for the experts.

So many people had helped her out after they'd saved her life. She

36

didn't know most of them by name because a lot of the work of creating a new identity went on in the background. Taking a silly risk to look up someone she was never supposed to see again seemed rude and dismissive of their efforts.

It had taken more than a year after she'd woken from her coma before she was healthy enough to leave the facility. They'd wanted her walking on her own steam and to be able to hold down a job before letting her out.

Her physical therapists had become the closest people to her, but she'd remained a job to them. It had taken years to build a life around the Tess persona and now it was all at risk.

She considered calling John Tynan, the Marshal in charge of her case. And rejected it again. A promise to Flynn meant a lot to her. He'd been so angry when he'd seen her. She knew much of that had been shock and hurt. And she didn't blame him a bit. She'd lied through omission to the best friend she'd ever had. He'd probably never truly forgive her for that.

Ginger knocked over the jar and Tessa smiled. "Sorry. There's nothing in there at all. If you come with me back to the lodge, I'll get you some food."

A peek at her phone showed she had enough time to do her stretches before climbing into the canoe. It was chilly in the cabin, but she didn't bother stoking the stove. No point in wasting the fuel when she had to leave soon.

Tessa shoved off the couch and groaned as she straightened. She'd tried sleeping on the bed that rested against the southern wall of the cabin, but she hadn't been able to stay there. Not with thoughts of Flynn joining her in the bed. The fantasies had blended with regrets and worries. And fear.

Ginger yowled again, making Tessa laugh. She started her stretching routine. "You're stuck with me for a bit. Then we're going to get in the canoe together. We should be early enough to get into the lodge and get some food for both of us before we meet Flynn."

The whole time she stretched, she spoke to the cat, trying to get her used to her voice and presence. Hopefully she would let Tessa pick her up when it was time to leave.

Leaving the cat hiding in the cabin would be fine, except she'd have to head right back out after her conversation with Flynn with some food. She didn't want to leave Ginger outdoors. It was almost December and she was afraid the tiny body would freeze.

Once her own body was loose enough to move normally, Tessa packed her few items in her backpack and slid it on. "Come on, Ginger. Time to go. We'll get you some food at the lodge."

Ginger didn't appear to believe her and skittered under the bed. Tessa couldn't get down on the floor to entice the cat. It would be too difficult to climb to her feet again and the cat would simply escape.

After twenty minutes, she moved and opened the door a crack. "Last chance, Ginger. I have to leave. I'm already late."

She didn't want Flynn to think she'd taken off on him. When the cat made no move to appear, she sighed. "I'll be back with food. Don't destroy anything."

It was going to be a very long day.

Tessa maneuvered herself into the canoe. The water was high enough she could drop into it from the dock. She'd learned the pattern of how to get to a sitting position on the dock and then use the pilings to balance as she dropped to the canoe seat. Not in the least bit graceful, but effective.

As she untied the canoe, she looked up to see Ginger watching her from a window beside the door. "Sorry, I'm not abandoning you. I will be back. You should have come with me, silly girl."

With a sigh, Tessa pushed off the dock and turned toward the lodge. She hadn't checked the temperatures, but it was definitely below freezing. More ice would be forming on the lake edges today. She'd have to add the data to her app later. Stopping to do it now would make her even later.

Unless she needed to leave. Abandon her turtles and her data. And her friends. Her heart ached as it had all night with the thought of losing everything she'd gained.

The faintest tinge of dawn was brightening the eastern horizon when she rounded a bend and saw the lodge. It was early, but there were still several lights shining. Tansy didn't follow the regular sleep patterns of most humans. When she was deep into a project, she could easily go more than a day without breaking for anything but the barest of essentials.

After one night of next to no sleep, Tessa's brain was thick and heavy. Or maybe that was her heart.

The exercise had helped to warm her upper body, but her legs were still stiff when she was close enough to see the dock. She paddled in and brought herself to the pilings she used to tie up. She exchanged the paddle for the rope and threw it around the first piling.

"Didn't think you were going to show."

Tessa yelped but managed not to topple the canoe as Flynn emerged from the shadows of the dock above her. Her heart raced but she steadied her fingers and tied the rope. When she reached to tie the second rope, Flynn took it out of her hand and did it for her.

She'd hoped to be out of the canoe and on equal footing with Flynn when they spoke. The stubborn cat had cost her the time. Tessa put her backpack on the dock and rose slowly, keeping the canoe steady. She tried to ignore the strong and virile man standing above her.

With a deep breath, she placed both hands flat on the dock and bent her knees to push off the bottom of the small boat. Today, she needed to get this on the first try.

Her legs didn't want to cooperate, but she pushed through the stiffness and lifted herself. Not enough. Her body started back down, when suddenly strong hands reached under her arms and pulled her up smoothly.

When she was high enough, Flynn set her down on the dock gently. At least the sun wasn't up and he couldn't see the embarrassment flushing her skin. She nodded her thanks, but wasn't able to speak.

The fluidness of the man's strength staggered her. She'd never been strong or particularly athletic, but the injuries she'd sustained had taken even that meager skill level away.

"Why don't we go inside and talk?" His deep baritone rumbled through her, complete with an edge of pity.

"I'm fine here. I don't want to risk anyone overhearing this."

Flynn sighed. "Fine. I think we tell everyone we met somewhere else. It's too hard to hide the fact that we know each other. We can say it was at school or something. No one has to know anything else."

"How much did you tell Sam?"

His hesitation was enough to tell her he'd said too much. "I didn't have to say a lot. He figured it out."

That was impossible to believe. "Not without help."

Flynn shifted. "He saw both of our reactions when you arrived last night. It was impossible to hide the shock. He guessed you were in hiding or Wit Sec. Then he put it together with the story I'd told him before of your house exploding back in high school."

That made her shudder. Even thinking about that time was enough to give her nightmares for days.

"Sam's a former FBI agent and as smart as they come. He also understands the seriousness of keeping your identity secret."

"Why did you tell him about that day?"

She couldn't see much of his expression but he shrugged. "I work in the Organized Crime unit at the FBI. We talk cases sometimes."

Tessa couldn't stop the flinch. This was bad. Very bad. "You've looked into the explosion from back then? You were a kid when that happened. But you've looked into it from work? It's still an open case?" The questions spilled out of her and she heard her voice shake.

Flynn reached out to her, but she stepped back, careful not to get close to the edge of the dock.

Panic roared through her system. "They'll know you're investigating. They'll have eyes on you. It's too dangerous. If they find out I've ever been here, they'll get a hold of you. They'll torture you for information. They'll hurt you. I can't stay. I have to leave. They can't get you. They can't find any connection to me here."

Her voice shook and every part of her wanted to roll into a ball and cry. Just by being here at Midnight Lake, she'd put a target on Flynn's back. She pushed past him and hurried to the lodge.

Time to leave.

lynn shook his head to get his brain to work.

It wasn't yet bright enough to see Tessa's face clearly, but the complete panic in her voice had him reeling. As did her words. She wasn't afraid for herself. Well, she probably was, but she was more scared for him and the other people here. When had anyone other than family put their own safety after his?

Her gait was stiff and awkward as she tried to hurry. Not something she'd been affected by when they were younger. She'd also struggled to get out of the canoe and onto the dock. Had she been injured?

It only took a few strides for Flynn to catch her. When he touched her arm, she flinched back as if he'd grabbed her.

"It's okay, Tessa. Relax. No one knows I'm here."

She shook her head and moved up the stairs to the deck. "It's too big a risk. It's too dangerous. I'm not putting you in danger. I'm not putting anyone else on their radar. Forget you ever saw me."

Tessa pulled open the door and Jetson immediately rose to his feet. He barked softly and moved to Tessa's side. She reached down and patted his head. "It's okay, Jetson. It's okay."

It obviously wasn't. Jetson looked at Flynn, as if to assess whether he had a solution or whether he was the problem. Flynn wasn't entirely sure. He only knew he wasn't ready to let Tessa walk out of his life. He didn't want to lose her again either.

At the bottom of the stairs, Tessa took a deep breath and then moved up. Everything about her body language and voice said panic, but her body moved slowly.

She'd blurted out that she was afraid he would be tortured for information. Had she been tortured? There was so much he didn't know. So much he needed to know.

Flynn followed her up the stairs to her room and moved inside before she could lock him out. Tessa didn't even look at him. She moved to the tiny closet and pulled out a couple of duffle bags. One was already full. A Go Bag?

She placed them both on the bed and unzipped the empty one. When she yanked open a drawer in a dresser that looked to be a century old, he moved to stand beside her. "Please don't do this. Sit down for a minute and let's talk this through."

"I can't. There's no time. When they follow up to see why you're here, I need to be gone. They can't make any connection between us or they'll kill you. Or worse. I can't risk you. I can't risk the people here. I need to go."

Her obvious panic had him striking the possibility of her being a mole off the table. No one was that good of an actress.

Which meant she was still his Cat. Tess. Tessa. He couldn't lose her after having just found her. His hurt feelings that she hadn't contacted him faded away as he realized she'd been following the rules to keep him safe.

"Tessa, we can not only protect you here, we can work together to take them down."

Her head was shaking before he even got three words in. "They're too big. Too powerful. Too evil. I can't lead them to you. To any of you."

She was shoving everything from her drawers into the duffle. "Please leave. I need to do something private." Then she stopped and her laugh was shaky and harsh. "I guess it doesn't matter anymore."

In the closet, she did something to a sheet of panelling and it slid soundlessly backward a couple of inches. Tessa pushed it to the side, revealing a tiny space. Large enough for her to hide in.

She reached in and grabbed a pouch then closed the panel. Not only did she have a prepared Go Bag, but a secret room and probably fake IDs in the bag.

Flynn stepped into her as she moved to put the pouch in her bag. She hadn't raised her face to him since they'd been on the dock and he needed her to see him, to truly listen to him past the fear. "Tessa."

She flinched at the name and a shudder ran through her.

"Tessa. We can figure this out, but you have to stay for us to do that. I want to help. I want to talk to you and get to know you all over again. Please, let me help."

When her head started to shake again, he couldn't stand it anymore. He stepped forward and wrapped her in his arms. Her entire body shuddered and she drew in a sharp breath of air.

Flynn kept his arms firm around her, even as he watched for signs of fear or tension. He'd let her go if she needed it. After another shudder, Tessa wrapped her arms around his waist and held on. She took deep steady breaths, possibly to keep in emotions. He did the same.

For long minutes, they stood wrapped around each other. Flynn wasn't sure he ever wanted to let her go. She felt exactly right where she was. And she was safe. At this exact moment, Flynn felt peace wrap around them both.

His doubts, worries, hurts were all gone. A sleepless night had brought him to the conclusion that he'd been a jerk to Tessa the day before. He should have done *this* right away. Held her, told her he'd missed her, that she was important.

"I'm sorry I was an ass yesterday. Apparently, I don't do well with big shocks. I'm so glad you're alive. I've missed you every damn day and I don't want to lose you again. Please give me a chance to help."

She shuddered again and Flynn held her more closely, rested his cheek on the top of her hair.

"I don't want anyone getting hurt because of me."

The sadness in her voice melted something inside of him. "First, none of this is because of you. Unless you're the kingpin of the crime family, hiding out here to lure in random FBI agents."

He regretted the flippant words immediately, but Tessa snorted out a half laugh and squeezed him. "That's right. I blew myself into a coma to throw you off the scent."

Coma?

That word had Flynn finally thinking about the situation from Tessa's point of view. His feelings had been hurt because she hadn't contacted him, because he'd spent years thinking she was dead.

She'd been alone since the moment of the explosion. In reality, she'd been alone most of her life. And he'd almost let her slip away without even thinking about it from her perspective. She'd lost everything that day. Her home, her family—such as they were—her identity. The rest of senior year in high school. The schooling she'd wanted to pursue. Her future.

He was a selfish, self-absorbed bastard. And that was changing. Now.

While they held each other, he organized his thoughts. Strangely, her touch made it easier to see things clearly. "No one at the office knows where I am. They know I'm on vacation. A few of them know I've gone up north to see about a business opportunity and to spend time with friends. I'm not sure I've even said Vermont, but certainly nothing more specific than that."

She nodded into his chest to show she'd heard, but didn't respond otherwise.

"Midnight Lake is probably one of the best places in the world to hide. Not only does it require that two-mile hike in, but the security is about as strong as it can be in the middle of a forest."

She nodded again.

"Let's take some time to figure this out, Tessa. I won't let them get to you."

She lifted her head and finally looked at him. "It's not me I'm worried about. They're evil, Flynn. I can't let them hurt anyone I care about."

Her eyes were haunted and Flynn knew the fear was justified. Criminal organizations were known for their cruelty and ruthlessness.

"Will you let me try to help Tessa? Will you give us some time to figure this out? All of it?"

She studied him with serious eyes for a long moment. When she finally nodded, relief and victory filled him.

Now he just had to make sure they all stayed alive.

CHAPTER 6

Can You Keep A Secret?

Tessa wondered if she'd lost her mind. She should be running. Well, actual running was beyond her ability level, but she should be already on the trail to the sawmill where she should jump in her car and drive without looking back.

Instead, she was holding onto Flynn and breathing in his strength right along with his scent. Her body had always reacted when Flynn was near. She'd even felt a warm shiver of awareness when she'd spotted the silhouettes on the dock, before she knew it was him.

He'd been such a good person when they were in high school. Hard-working, confident, friendly. He'd been an outstanding athlete in school and had excelled at rodeo.

Instead of being the stereotypical jock who acted superior, he'd been nice to everyone. They'd got to know each other over math problems and had become friends. She thought they'd maybe been edging toward more. Although that might have just have been her who'd been thinking about kisses and love.

Back then, she'd considered telling him what worried her about her family. Would that have changed anything? Impossible to know.

Finally, Tessa drew in another deep breath and nodded again. She was going to take a leap of faith and trust him. "I can't promise to stay indefinitely, but if no one knows specifically where you are, you should be safe."

He frowned down at her. "*We. We* should be safe."

In the grand scheme of things, Tessa knew she didn't matter much. She didn't have family worrying about her, didn't have people to mourn her if she died. Her grandfather might have ordered the explosion that had been aimed at killing her and her father and uncle. Tessa had no memories of her mother, but she hoped at least Rosa had loved her baby.

She'd been building a new family here at Midnight Lake over the past few weeks. She didn't want to abandon this life, but she would if it kept them all safe. For now, she'd follow her heart and not her head.

She picked up the bag with the different identification cards and emergency phone in it. She shouldn't have opened the secret space in front of him, but she'd planned on leaving. Although, if there was one person in the world she trusted, it was Flynn.

When she moved into the closet, she wasn't surprised to find he followed her and peeked over her shoulder when she opened the secret panel.

"Very James Bond. I like it. Is it part of the original lodge, or did you do it?"

"I had Aisling make it for me."

"That must have been fun for her. Not everyone gets the chance to make a secret room."

Tessa smiled. "She loved doing it." Although she'd been worried at the need, she hadn't pestered her with questions when Tessa had said it was probably silly, but it would make her feel safer.

"Smart to make it big enough for you to be inside. I hope you haven't had to use it."

She shook her head. "No. If I had, I would have left as soon as it was safe."

He nodded and his expression turned serious. "I'm glad you didn't."

She managed a small smile. "Me too."

"I really did miss you, Tessa. I know this is a mess right now, but I'm so glad to see you again. I want to find a solution that doesn't involve you leaving."

So did she, but saying it aloud might jinx it.

A knock at the door had them both turning. Tansy's voice called out softly. "Hey, Tessa. It's me. Everything okay?"

Was it? She had no idea. Instead of saying that, she opened the door and smiled at her friend. "Hi. I'm okay."

Jetson stood from where he'd been lying on the floor and walked over to Tessa to nuzzle her hand. She immediately petted the dog.

Tansy patted his back. "I found Jetson in front of your door and he wouldn't come with me. I wanted to make sure you were okay."

Tessa knelt down and wrapped the dog in a hug. "Thanks, Jetson. I'm good."

Tansy nodded but looked between her and Flynn.

Hugging the dog reminded Tessa of Ginger. "I have to go back to the cabin. I left the stray cat inside and she's probably destroyed half the place looking for food. Maybe Jetson can come with me in the canoe. What do you think boy, would you like that?"

Jetson licked her face and she laughed.

"Mind if I come along?"

Flynn's voice had her turning to look up at him. It would be a good place to talk. Private. No worry about being overheard. No fear of strangers finding them.

"That's a good idea." Tessa started to straighten and Tansy moved in immediately to support her on one side. Flynn picked up on the cue and had her other arm before she could tell them both she was fine. It was much easier to stand with their assistance, so she nodded her thanks instead. Even if her face was flaming.

Flynn squeezed her arm gently then let go. "Let me just grab my things. I'll be right back."

When they were alone, Tansy moved in more closely. "Are you okay? How can I help? What do you need?"

Tears filled Tessa's eyes but she blinked them away and squeezed Tansy's hands. "That means more than you'll ever know. I don't know what I'm going to do. I have to talk to Flynn and figure things out."

"You can ask me for anything. I'll help however I can. So will the others."

And this was exactly why she didn't want to leave. For the first time since waking up in a hospital, she had a home, friends who were becoming family. "I'll let you know when I figure it out."

Tansy reached forward and pulled her into a hug. Then she whispered. "I can see the chemistry crackling between you two. But I can have the CleanySaurs take him out if you need them to do that."

Tessa laughed, knowing it was a joke to lighten the mood. "I'll keep that in mind."

Tessa moved her fully packed bags into the closet, knowing Tansy wouldn't miss the fact that they were ready to go. She grabbed her workbag that included her tablet and her phone. "Do we have any food that might interest a scared cat?"

"Let's go see what we can find."

Flynn paddled from the back of the canoe where he could keep an eye on Tessa. The shadows under her eyes were heavy and she'd struggled to stand from kneeling to comfort the dog.

Tansy's response had been instinctive, almost as if she expected it. Added to Tessa's struggle to get out of the canoe and her slow ascent of the stairs, he wanted to know exactly what physical difficulties she had. And he wanted to know why.

Hell, he wanted to know everything.

She paddled smoothly and easily. Turning back to Jetson, who sat in the middle like he was the King of the Lake, didn't cause her any difficulty with balance or movement.

What was wrong with her legs? And was it related to the explosion?

They didn't hurry to the cabin, but they didn't dawdle either. The air was heavy and Flynn wondered if that's how it felt when snow was expected.

He'd been too preoccupied the night before to pay attention to his surroundings. In the morning light, he realized it was gorgeous. Not at all like the ranch back in Texas, but beautiful all the same. The lake was twisty and unpredictable. The leaves had dropped off the deciduous trees, but there were enough conifers to fill the space, keeping it from being bare.

He'd assumed winter in the woods would feel and look lonely. It was anything but. The few inches of snow made it appear cozy and somehow intimate. He wondered how it would feel when those inches changed into feet. And if he would be there to see it.

Would Tessa?

There had to be a way to convince her to stay. He wasn't sure if pulling her into his investigation was the best way to do that or if that would send her running.

Flynn didn't want to endanger her, but he was confident in the ability of the team around them. They could keep her safe. No one was going to do anything to risk her. It was his job to convince her of that and get her to stay here with her friends. And him.

When they pulled up to the dock in front of the cabin where she'd stayed the night before, they each tied a rope to a piling. Jetson jumped to the dock. Flynn followed suit and then moved to the front of the boat and offered his hands to Tessa.

She studied him for a long moment and he waited her out.

Finally she gave a small nod and lifted her arms. He lifted her up and set her on her feet. She stepped back immediately with another nod. Even though he didn't want to let her go, he did.

Every second he spent with her reminded him of the growing feelings he'd felt as a teen. A teen wondering if what he was feeling was simply friendship mixed with lust or whether it was the bigger L word.

He couldn't lose her again. Couldn't let her go without exploring that. If she had to disappear for her safety, he could go with her. It would be a temporary solution. A way to keep her safe until they figured out the future. Hopefully, it wouldn't come to that.

Jetson woofed softly and Flynn looked up to spot the cat staring at them from the window. There'd always been barn cats on the ranch, and this one looked as pissed off as any he'd seen. Maybe bringing along the dog hadn't been such a great idea.

Tessa reached into the bag she'd packed with enough food for a dozen cats and chose a jar filled with rice and cooked veggies.

From his experience, cats preferred meat, but there wasn't a lot of that at the lodge. As a Texan, Flynn wasn't sure how he felt about that. There was really nothing as good as a thick grilled steak.

Tessa turned to Jetson and pointed at the cat. "This is Ginger. You make sure Ginger stays inside when we open the door, okay? We don't want to scare her away. We want to keep Ginger safe."

The dog looked from Tessa to the cat and back, panting happily.

The name she'd chosen for her cat slammed into him and he nearly missed his cue to step through the door before Tessa closed it behind them.

She was already speaking to the cat and holding out the food. "Hi, Ginger. I've got food for you. And a couple of new friends. Well, you met Flynn last night, I guess. This is Jetson. He won't hurt you."

As she continued to talk softly, she moved to sit on the chair and put the jar of food on the floor by her feet.

Flynn struggled with his emotions. Tessa hadn't forgotten him or his family. She'd chosen her name because of them. And she'd named this stray cat after the horse she'd ridden that day on his ranch.

He'd been so pissed when he'd first realized she was alive and hadn't let him know. Now he was humbled by the tributes she'd paid to him and his family. He would keep her safe. No matter the cost.

The orange whirlwind bounced off every surface of the room even as she moved in closer to the food and skittered back. Jetson sat beside the door and followed every move with his gaze. Ears up and alert, he seemed to be enjoying the cat's antics.

Finally, Ginger snagged a bite of the food and then bounced back with a hiss.

She looked from Tessa to the food to Jetson and to him. Then back to the food. No one moved, Tessa kept talking softly, and eventually the cat came back again and again.

When the jar was empty, she knocked it over with her paw and scooted under the bed that stood against the side wall. Jetson tilted his head then laid his head on his paws with a yawn.

"All the cat's activity wear you out, buddy?" Flynn scratched the dog's head, then he moved to fire up the pellet stove. It was freezing in the cabin.

Tessa closed up the jar and returned it to her bag. "Do you know anything about cats? How long should I wait before I feed her again?"

Flynn shrugged. "Most of the cats who lived in the barn fed themselves on mice and whatever else they could catch. I imagine her belly's full right now. Probably stay that way for a few hours at least."

Which meant they had a few hours to talk. Flynn knew it was going to be a difficult conversation for both of them. He put the kettle on the stove and then sat in the chair opposite Tessa at the table.

While she'd been worried about getting food for the cat back at the lodge, Flynn had raided the fridge for the two of them. Apparently Jetson would be fine until the evening, but he'd brought some of his food just in case. Sam had been in the kitchen and mentioned that Tess probably hadn't eaten the night before because she'd planned to be back at the lodge for his welcome meal.

Flynn pulled out a container of homemade blueberry muffins. He didn't have a clue who the baker in the group was, but they smelled delicious. He also had some cheese and fruit. Not bacon and eggs, but not a bad breakfast. With good company. "So, do you want me to start, or would you rather go first?"

Tessa frowned slightly at him. "I'd rather avoid the entire discussion, but I guess that's not an option."

"Not if we want you to stay at Midnight Lake. And we do."

If she was right about the Pavics monitoring him, he'd brought danger to her door. He needed to fix it.

CHAPTER 7

Spilling The Beans

Tessa gripped her hands in her lap and nodded, but she couldn't make eye contact with Flynn. "I'll go first. If I'm going to tell you, I'd rather just blurt it out."

Flynn nodded and leaned forward and placed his elbows on the table, all of his attention focused on her. Too bad it was because he wanted her story. Not her.

The bed was at her back and she was glad she'd chosen her seat first. Having Flynn in front of her was making her want all kinds of things. Some things she'd never had a chance to experience. Seeing the bed behind him would be too much. And she was focusing on her attraction to the man in order to avoid talking about the hard stuff.

She closed her eyes to focus, then opened them. "What do you want to know?"

"Everything."

His expression showed he was serious. He already knew a lot about her past. Telling him the rest and the after-effects wasn't going to change much. She could still disappear if she needed to do that.

"Okay. My first memory after the explosion is of waking up in a hospital room. I didn't know it at the time, but the room was in a secured basement below a hospital in Dallas."

"Dallas?"

"They'd moved me. It was months before I knew that they'd told people I hadn't survived when the house blew up." It had taken her a while to remember who she was and that the explosion had even happened.

"How did you survive?"

That was a time she didn't like to remember. "Apparently I was blown out the window and bounced a time or two before landing in the pool. I landed on some debris and more landed on top of me. The water put out the fire and the debris stopped me from drowning."

Flynn swore harshly. "That's horrible. Do you know what caused the explosion?"

She frowned up at him. "I rarely got answers when I asked any questions, so I eventually stopped asking. I assume it was one of my father's competitors."

"Do you know what business your father was in?"

The familiar ache started in her gut. Was this another person who wouldn't believe her? Another person who would look at her like she was nothing but a liar?

"We were never close. As I got older, I wondered if he was into something illegal, along with my grandfather and my uncle. My mother's brother." Below the table, she squeezed her hands together, a trick she'd learned to help her keep the words steady, so the interviewer wouldn't realize how his doubts affected her.

"What made you think that?"

She couldn't look at Flynn. "When I was little, we had a two-part assignment. We had to draw our parents at work and then draw ourselves at a job we wanted to do in the future. I realized I didn't know what my father did. When I asked him, he said it wasn't any of my damn business and that if my teacher wanted to keep her job, she'd better change the assignment."

"What did you do?"

"I drew him as a cowboy."

Flynn grinned but she couldn't. Anyone who knew where she'd lived would have known it was a lie. The house she'd lived in was fancy and maintained by staff. Not a horse or a bull in sight.

She'd kept quiet and worried about her teacher's job. And she'd kept right on worrying about her father. Tessa drew in a slow breath to quiet the familiar panic. "I never asked him again. He mostly ignored me, so that was easy."

"That sucks, Tessa. Did you ever find out anything else?"

Why was he digging so hard at this? Was he another one who thought she was a partner with her father?

But this was Flynn and she didn't have any real reason not to trust him yet. "Not really. But that last day, I came home from school to find my uncle in my room screaming that I'd betrayed them all. That I'd been giving details of their business to the cops. He was waving around a journal. It wasn't mine."

Her stomach and head ached. Jetson's head appeared in her lap and she unclenched her hands to pat the dog.

"Needless to say, no one believed me. They dragged me up to a room on the third floor and started to interrogate me." No need to go into the horrific details.

"Then there were a couple of booms and fire and screaming. The next memory I have is waking up in a hospital."

"When?"

She looked up to find his eyes piercing into hers. "What?"

"When did you wake up in that hospital bed?"

She turned back to Jetson. "At the end of August." Eight months after the house had exploded in December.

Flynn swore harshly. "I'm so sorry you went through that, Tessa. How injured were you?"

Her heart raced and she wanted to run, but she decided to finish it. It would be easier than having to go through it again. Flynn was the type to persist until he had all the answers he wanted. "The burns were mostly healed when I woke up. They'd also finished several surgeries to fix the worst of the broken bones."

Flynn shoved up from the table and paced around the tiny room. Jetson whined softly but stayed with her.

"How many surgeries?"

"I don't know. There were maybe ten surgeries after I woke up."

"Ten? Surgeries?" He squatted beside her and covered her hands with his. "I'm so damn sorry, Tessa."

"Not your fault."

His strong arms wrapped around her and she battled the urge to break down and sob. Crying didn't solve a damn thing. Big hands ran up and down her back and over her hair, offering her warmth and comfort.

Definitely not like the others who'd interviewed her.

Flynn shifted positions and scooped her up in his arms. He moved to the bed and settled back against the headboard with her on his lap.

She should probably move. Should probably protest that she was fine. That she was strong enough to handle this by herself.

But she didn't.

She didn't want to be strong enough. Didn't want to be alone. Instead of pushing away, she leaned into Flynn's chest and let his strength rush through her.

Jetson hopped up on the bed and snuggled in, resting his head on her lap.

Tessa couldn't remember ever feeling so safe.

Flynn held Tessa as he battled his demons.

He was an ass. He'd been so pissed at her. And exactly none of it was her fault.

In a coma for months. Eight months. Over a dozen surgeries to fix whatever had broken during the explosion and fall.

Never mind dealing with finding herself being accused of betrayal by her uncle and interrogated. What the hell did that even mean? Had they tortured her?

When Jetson nudged his hand, Flynn managed to regulate his breathing again. Tessa was relaxing against him. Her breathing smoothing out and the tension easing from her body.

He needed to do the same. Remind himself she was alive. Strong enough to make a new life for herself. Strong enough to thrive despite the hell she'd been through. He didn't want that taken from her.

Was it possible anyone *was* following his travel? Checking him out? Would he lead them to her? Until now, he hadn't thought that was an actual possibility. Now, he thought it might be and he needed to ensure that didn't happen.

He thought she might have fallen asleep when she spoke again. "My new life story is that I grew up on a farm southwest of Salina, Kansas. My parents, Robert and Gloria died when a tornado destroyed the area. I have a zoology degree from the University of Wyoming."

"Why zoology?"

"According to the rules, I had to choose something different from what had appealed to me in my old life. I was pretty apathetic at the time and when someone suggested zoology, I went along with it. I like it more than I expected."

"Even canoeing in the winter?"

Her chuckle was soft. "Even that. It's peaceful. And the patterns and numbers are there, just not the way I'd expected them to be. Trying to discover patterns over time and figure out how we humans can learn from the animals is interesting."

Obviously, resiliency was not an issue for Tessa. Her love of learning probably helped her with that.

Her whisper was barely audible. "I'm afraid I'm going to lose Tessa if I keep focusing on the past."

He kissed her hair and ran his hands over her in comfort. "We won't let that happen."

Although he didn't know if he could promise that. "How much does the marshal in charge of your case know about your past?"

"I assume he knows everything. Why?"

"Just thinking it all through. Trying to figure out the best way to move forward."

A shudder ran through her. "By using me as bait to draw out my grandfather and stop his organization?"

He squeezed her firmly against him even as Jetson snuggled in closer. "No. We're not putting you at risk. But maybe there's a way to end this. If we put what I know together with what you know, maybe we can see a way out."

"I don't know much."

She probably knew more than she thought. She was observant and intelligent. While she'd pushed away the memories, she might know enough to help him close the case.

Then he could move on. Out of the FBI and onto Midnight Security. With Tessa right here with him.

Flynn kept his hand moving up and down her back, skimming from her hair to her waist. Soft curls, lithe body. He forced his body not to react by envisioning Tessa being tossed out a window while she was burning.

Holding her felt right. Being with her felt right.

She sighed but didn't raise her head. "Your turn. Tell me about you."

"What?"

"I told you my sordid story. Tell me how you ended up as an FBI agent and not a rodeo star or horse trainer."

She remembered his dreams. "I mostly work out of the Houston office, so I still get to help on the ranch and with any kids wanting to ride the bulls and broncs."

"You always loved the connections with those animals."

He chuckled. "Except when the brahma's horns connected."

She laughed softly.

It took a few moments to organize his thoughts. "Everything changed that day. They couldn't tell us answers. They couldn't tell us who'd attacked your family or even who'd been inside the house. The only person they identified was you."

Tessa shoved up to look at him, shock obvious on her face. "What? What about my father and my uncle? The others?"

He shook his head. "They said there were two males burned beyond recognition. No one else was found in the debris. The men were presumed to be your father and uncle but no positive identifications were made."

Tessa blinked and stared at him. He felt her trembling before she shoved off his lap to back away toward the table. "Are you sure that's what they said? Who said? The police? The press?"

"I'm sure. That's what was reported to the press by the police. There was a press conference." How did she not know all this? Hadn't they told her anything when they'd moved her into Wit Sec?

She was completely spooked and Flynn wanted to pull her back into his arms. He could see her hands trembling as she used them to shove back her hair.

Her wide eyes finally met his. "But it's not true. Is any of it true?"

Flynn didn't have a clue. The only part he'd believed had turned out to be false.

"What if they're not dead?" Her strangled whisper had him swinging his feet off the side of the bed and reaching for her. She shook her head and backed up.

"Slow down, honey. Don't panic. You're safe. No one knows where you are. No one can get to you. We're safe here."

She shook her head slowly. "You don't know that. You can't."

"You're right. I've doubted parts of the story my whole life. The only part I believed was that you'd been killed. I'm glad that part's not true, but it makes me wonder what else isn't true. How many people were in the house with you?"

Tessa closed her eyes and blew out a few breaths, obviously trying to bring her panic under control. She walked slowly around the small cabin, closing the curtains against the night. "I came home to five men in my room that day. Including my father and uncle."

"Did you recognize the others?" The bastards who'd interrogated her. He didn't know what that meant yet but he wanted them to never see the light of day again.

Her head shake was sharp. "I'd never met them before. I always stayed in my room when my father had meetings."

"Can you walk me through that day with more detail? It's important."

Every drop of color leeched from Tessa's face and she dropped into a chair.

"Afterward, I wondered if there was a sixth person, or if there were hidden cameras I didn't know about. My uncle seemed to know I was coming up the stairs. He said something like *Here she comes now* when I was out of sight down the hall. I think he placed the journal in my room and then pulled it out dramatically to prove to my father that I was ratting him out."

She blew out a breath. "Not that I even know now exactly what business he was involved in. Whatever my uncle had in the book had my father convinced. I'd never seen him that furious."

Her hands twisted together on the table, knuckles white. "The first punch to my jaw took me completely by surprise. I'd never been hit in my life. There were more hits and kicks."

Flynn gripped the bed below him to keep himself still. Her voice was thick and barely audible.

"I was only half conscious when my uncle told the other men to take me to the interrogation room. I didn't even know it existed. Up on the third floor behind multiple locks."

"They threw me on the floor and two of the men stayed in the room. My uncle said they could do whatever they wanted to me."

Her body shuddered and Flynn couldn't stop the growl. Jetson bounded off the bed and moved to her again.

Tessa's hands ran over his fur. The orange cat hopped onto the table from wherever she'd been hiding and sat watching her. One of Tessa's hands moved to her, but she stayed out of reach. With a sigh, she went back to petting Jetson.

"The two of them argued for a while. I couldn't make sense of it. My head was ringing and I was trying to figure out what was happening and how to get away."

"One man punched the other guy and tossed him out of the room. Then he picked me up and threw me onto a bed. He was undoing his pants when the house exploded."

Relief filled him. On top of everything else, she wasn't having to cope with being raped as well.

He couldn't stay away from her any more. He squatted on the other side of the chair from Jetson and patted her hair with one hand and her arm with the other. "Hell, Tessa. I can't imagine how utterly terrified you had to be. That's one of the most horrific things I've ever heard. I'm so damn sorry you went through that."

His own voice broke and Tessa turned to him, her eyes brimming with tears. Flynn pulled her into his arms and held her when she broke into sobs. He cradled her in his arms and returned them to the bed. Once again she snuggled in.

Her tears were fierce but they didn't last long. "I'm sorry."

He let the emotion show in his voice. "Nothing to be sorry for, Tessa. I'm skating a thin edge here and it didn't happen to me. Emotions only explode at the worst times when you keep them inside. Let them out and then you start to heal."

She looked up at him with tears on her cheeks. "That's pretty smart."

"It should be. It's a direct quote from the therapist I saw after that day. My family was great, but Dr. Perez was the one who got me through it. She helped me find ways to channel my anger and grief. Helped me realize that rodeo wasn't the future I wanted any more."

"What did you want?"

"I wanted to take down the bastards who'd hurt you."

CHAPTER 8

Second Time Around

Tessa hugged Flynn even more tightly. He'd changed his plans and his dreams because of her. Because he thought she was dead and he'd wanted to find the men who'd set the explosions that had killed her.

Could she love this man any more? "You're a good man, Flynn Walker."

He flinched and she lifted her head to see him frowning and shaking his head. She lifted a finger and touched his lips to stop him from speaking. "You are. You always were the best person I knew when I was a kid and I've seen nothing to indicate that's changed."

His frown didn't disappear. "No, I'm not, Tessa. I was so pissed off when I saw you in that canoe. I thought you'd walked away from me and hidden yourself away because you didn't care."

Her body stiffened and she thought about moving away from his touch, but his lopsided, sad grin stopped her. "Obviously, I got over that. I was thinking from the viewpoint of a selfish teenage boy. I was so shocked to see you, my emotions went into overdrive. That's not an excuse, just the truth. It took a sleepless night and maybe a conversation or two with you and Sam to get my head on straight."

His frown disappeared and he smiled softly. "I lost you once through no fault of our own. I don't want to lose you again."

Tessa's heart swelled and she didn't bother to resist her desire. She leaned forward and pressed her lips softly to Flynn's. Then she whispered. "See. The best man I know."

With a growl that sent shivers of the very best kind over her body, he captured her lips. And most of her brain cells. She leaned into the kiss and Flynn growled again. His hands drifted up her body to cup her face.

His lips were tender and the kiss was gentle. So sweet, she knew she could cry from it.

For long moments, they nipped and sipped, touched and learned. When Flynn slowed and broke the kiss, she leaned back enough to see his face. His smile made her feel lighter, more whole.

"I've been wanting to do that since you sat beside me in math. Never thought I'd have the chance."

Tessa raised an eyebrow. "Seriously?"

His eyes twinkled. "Seriously. I was planning to ask you to go to the Christmas dance with me that day."

She refused to let the awful memories distract her from this good one. "I would have said yes. I would have said yes to almost anything."

This time it was Flynn's eyebrows shooting up. A grin lit up his face. "Good to know. I had a pretty sleepless night back then wondering if you'd agree to be my girlfriend."

That made her laugh. "You? Nervous? You were the hotshot rodeo star and had every girl in the school wanting to be your date."

"The only one I wanted was you."

Her eyes told her he was serious and a thrill ran through her. She hadn't made the attraction bigger than it had been in order to get through those painful days. He'd really been interested in her nerdy self.

He still was.

They moved at the same time as their lips met in a collision that was less gentle and more demanding.

Without breaking the kiss, Tessa shifted so that she was straddling Flynn as best as her legs would allow her. He growled at the intimate contact and her body reacted to how he'd hardened beneath her.

Flynn's hands moved to her hips and squeezed, then had her

moving, grinding against him. She gasped into the kiss as the sensations filled her.

She ran her fingers up his chest, savoring the muscles beneath his shirt and the strength they implied. Her body never felt strong and she wanted to absorb all that she could from Flynn because the man was strong in all senses of the word.

Flynn broke the kiss and his mouth traveled along her jawline. Her head dropped back of its own accord to give him better access.

Her hands moved over his chest and shoulders, enjoying his reaction to her touch. Every few moments, their lips came together again and again. Each touch built the need and the desire until every part of Tessa was shaking with it.

Flynn's hands skimmed her ribcage, brushing the sides of her breasts and making her body spiral even tighter. He groaned into her mouth and then he pulled back and rested his forehead against hers. "Holy hell, Tessa, you're potent."

His breathing was harsh and ragged. Her own was no better, but knowing he was as affected as she was made her feel powerful. She smiled. "You too."

His returning smile was full of tenderness and she knew she'd have to tell him.

Tessa felt her face flush, but she forced herself to maintain eye contact. She was an adult and she would act like one. "I've never been this close with a man before."

Flynn's body reacted instantly. His entire body tightened and his hands flexed where they'd been resting on her hips. "What?"

Her flush deepened but she kept her head up. "I spent a couple of years living in the basement of that hospital. I needed the surgeries and recuperation times and then I needed to learn to walk again."

Flynn frowned but his hands started moving again. Gently. Tenderly.

"Then I spent at least six months in the towns and cities from my new biography. I'm not a good actress, so I needed to know the places they'd given me in my new background. I had a different last name for those years, but I was already working on making myself into Tessa."

Flynn shook his head softly. "I can't imagine how incredibly difficult that was."

"It was fine. I just want to explain why I'm so inexperienced at this."

His grin was immediate and his eyes twinkled. "Well, so far, I can say you're doing very well. A+."

Even while she was embarrassed by the conversation, he could make her laugh.

She blew out a deep breath and he tapped her on the nose. "It's okay, Tessa. We're not in a race. We're not going to do anything you're not comfortable with. It's not like most people jump straight from a first kiss to sex. We'll take our time. Enjoy getting to know each other again."

"See. Best man ever."

Flynn rolled his eyes and squeezed her arms. "What else? I can see there's something else bothering you. Tell me." His soft voice was commanding and kind. A weird combination but it made this easier.

"There are scars. Lots and lots of scars."

"I guessed that from the number of surgeries."

She nodded. "Not just my legs, although those required the most work. My arms. My back. Wrists too."

His eyes were warm with concern. "I'm so sorry you've gone through all of that, Tessa. But scars only show that you're a survivor. That you're strong enough to keep moving forward. That you chose again and again and again to take the next step. If anyone thinks less of you because of that proof of your power, they're not worth your time."

The intensity of those brown eyes on hers convinced her he meant every word he said.

Then he gently lifted one of her hands in both of his. She wore a long sleeve shirt like she always did. Long pants and closed in shoes as well. Flynn ran his finger softly along the hem of the cuff. He looked to her for permission. When she nodded, he eased up the sleeve.

Most of the scars had faded over time, but they'd had to do several surgeries to repair her wrists so that her hands would function normally. The doctors said they'd been squashed in the fall.

"The major damage was mostly repaired by the time I woke up. They hadn't done the final surgeries while I was in the coma." Because they hadn't wanted to waste the time, effort, and expertise if she wasn't ever going to need her hands.

Flynn ran his finger over the scar tissue and then lifted her hand to kiss the area. He repeated the procedure with the other hand.

She was a quivering puddle of goo when he smiled at her.

"You're beautiful, Tessa. All of you. A few scars don't change that."

She didn't bother reminding him there were more than a few. He wouldn't care. And that not only amazed her, it hit her directly in the heart.

She'd always loved Flynn. He'd been her brightest light in a dim childhood. He'd been her friend and had brought her into his circle of friends, into his family. She'd loved him with all of her teenage heart.

And her heart hadn't changed its mind after all this time.

Flynn opened his eyes when Jetson let out a soft bark.

After Tessa had opened up about her scars and her virginity, they'd talked some more. Kissed some more. And then simply held each other until they drifted into a much needed nap after their sleepless night.

Waking with her wrapped in his arms felt surprisingly natural. She fit. They fit.

While they'd had a good couple of hours and had made progress in getting to know each other again, they really hadn't done any of the work needed to ensure she would be safe to stay at Midnight Lake.

To do that, he needed to take down the Pavic family.

Jetson barked again and Flynn turned to see what had the dog's interest. He spotted the cat sitting on top of Tessa's bag, pawing at the food jars inside.

When the cat knocked itself off the bag, his chuckle had Tessa stirring. She smiled and stretched against him, making sure his body was reacting properly. All systems go. Which reminded him she was a virgin. He told his body to slow the hell down and kissed her hair as chastely as he could.

The cat let out a yowl and Tessa leaned up to an elbow to look.

Ginger slapped her paw against the bag and then glared up at the humans.

Flynn stroked Tessa's hair. "I think your little Ginger is hungry again."

She laughed. "Now whatever gave you that idea?"

She pressed a quick kiss to his cheek and then sat up. Her movements were stiff and Flynn sat to swing out of the way, giving her an easy way to slide off the bed.

Even a decade after the explosion, the effects on her body were still evident. His heart ached for the pains she'd suffered. Having to learn to walk again. Living at a secured level in a hospital for more than a year.

Flynn wanted to give her a normal life. One where she wasn't looking over her shoulder. One where she didn't have to be afraid. She'd suffered so much and deserved more than what life had handed her. So much more.

"What if, between the two of us, we can take down the Pavic family? That would eliminate the worry for you. If we can get the leaders in jail, the threat to you would be over. They'd be powerless."

A shudder ran through her as she eased onto her feet. "We don't even know if anyone knows I'm alive. We don't know if there's a price on my head. This is all precautionary."

"The government rarely spends a lot of time or money on precautionary." And they'd spent a whole lot on her. They'd kept her in protective custody, paid for her to recover from the injuries, resettled her more than once.

When her face paled, he regretted his blunt words.

She turned to face him, ignoring the cat's demands. "Do you think they're using me as bait? Or is there another reason they kept me alive and hidden? Do you think the Pavic family is keeping me alive for some reason? Do you think they're involved with this? Are they working together?"

Her voice was shaking along with her body and Flynn moved to wrap her up in his arms. "Sorry, Tessa. I'm just thinking aloud. There's no way the government would work with Pavic. There's an open case file on them in the organized crime division. We've got no reason to go down the conspiracy route."

She drew in a few breaths. "Okay. Sorry. I've got to stop freaking out. I've kept it buried deep for so long. I haven't even let myself think of names or people. I haven't allowed my brain to revisit any of it. Now that the seal is broken, all the terror is leaking back out again. I'm sorry."

He shifted to frame her face with his hands. "There's nothing to be sorry about. That's on me. I've been working on this case for years and it's never far from the surface. I want to take them down. It's the only reason I haven't moved on."

Another shudder. "Moved on?"

He smiled. "To here. To Midnight Security with my friends. The opportunity is exciting. There's so much potential in what they've started. I want to be a part of it. But not until I close this case."

Tessa's eyes sparkled with tears. "For me." Then she threw her arms around him. "See. Best man ever."

"Not hardly." But that she'd said so more than once warmed his heart and gave him hope for an actual future with her.

Tessa straightened and moved to the bag she'd brought and took another jar out for the cat. It didn't move away from her when she opened the jar. Then it dove right in and didn't protest when Tessa ran her hands over the fur.

He wanted those hands running over his body just like that. Shaking his head at his one-track mind, Flynn forced his mind onto the case. He'd go slowly with Tessa, but he wasn't letting her go. Solving the case and dismantling the Pavic organization would go a long way to moving things in the right direction.

While the cat gobbled the food, Tessa sat on a nearby chair and continued to touch the animal, getting her used to her presence. Similar to the way they gentled abused horses back on the ranch. She was a natural with animals. Zoology had been a good second choice.

He moved to another chair at the table and pulled out the notebook he always carried with him when he traveled. A lot of his information was secured on a cloud in the computer, but he didn't know enough about computer hacking to be sure it was safe. If anyone stole the data, he'd be screwed. Better to have a paper copy as backup.

Plus, he thought better on paper when he was brainstorming. "You ready to dig into the Pavic family for a while?"

Her face clouded up, but she nodded.

He lifted a pen. "Why don't you tell me what you know?"

Her laugh held no humor. "It's a pretty short tale. My mother was Rosa Pavic. She died when I was very young. I don't have any memories of her and my father trained me early on never to ask about her."

Jesus. What a hell of a life she'd lived.

"My grandfather is Grigor. I've met him a few times. He's got eyes that look through you. His laugh makes my skin crawl. My mother's older brother is Karlo. He's the man who accused me of writing a journal about their family business."

The one who had set her up, hit her, and left her to be raped. That was the one Flynn wanted to see spend the rest of his life in a cell.

"I don't even know what types of crimes they're involved in. My father never allowed me out of my room when other people were in the home."

"You didn't look them up after you got into Wit Sec?" He wasn't sure he'd have been able to stop himself from checking them out.

Her mouth twisted. "I was told that there are ways for people to track me if I so much as searched for my previous name or anyone associated with it. If I'm being honest, those weren't the names I would have looked for if I'd been brave enough to search."

The way her eyes were locked on his made him think his name was the one she would have searched.

And that made him feel like he'd won the Calgary Stampede.

CHAPTER 9
Family Business

Tessa worried she was revealing too much to Flynn. He had always owned her heart and losing him the first time had nearly broken her.

Here she was, not even twenty-four hours into their second meeting and spinning fairy tales of love and forever in her mind. She should know better. She *did* know better. But those fairy tales refused to stop bubbling into existence.

Flynn believed if they could stop the Pavic family, she would be safe and so would the people around her. Was that true?

She didn't have any actual information to use against them. They shouldn't have wanted her dead or out of the way in the first place.

Why had her uncle set her up? Why had he wanted her out of the way? She hadn't known a single thing about whatever they were into.

The cat finished the food, and before she could dart away, Tessa scooped her up and settled her in her lap. An echo of how Flynn had comforted her. To her surprise, the cat kneaded her paws on Tessa's legs and then curled up into a ball.

Flynn chuckled. "Apparently food and kindness are the keys. Nicely done."

Tessa stroked the cat as she braced herself. "Your turn. Tell me what you know about the Pavic family." She didn't say *my family* because she didn't want to claim them.

She wasn't even sure she wanted to know what he was about to tell her. But if she wanted a chance at keeping Flynn in her life, she had to yank her head out of the sand.

Flynn nodded. "Once I managed to get assigned to the Organized Crime division, I started checking it out. From what we know, Grigor Pavic is the head of a small crime family."

"Small?"

He nodded. "They're not national and they stay mostly working around the Houston area. That's how they've stayed off the radar. Most of the division is focused on larger groups that regularly cross state lines."

"Okay. What kinds of things are they involved in?"

"It seems like they have interests in several areas. Gambling. Money laundering. Drugs. Prostitution. Anything that will bring in cash."

Tessa couldn't stop the shudder and the cat jumped off her lap. Ginger dashed toward the stove and bumped into Jetson. The dog licked the cat, making her jump again.

The two animals stared at each other. Finally, Ginger blinked and then plopped to sit near the dog.

Flynn raised an eyebrow. "That was pretty easy. I'd guess your Ginger spent some time with a family before she got lost in the woods. Or abandoned."

Tessa identified a little too much with the tiny cat. "How could any family be so awful?" Then she shook her head. "My father would never have allowed an animal in the house and wouldn't have thought twice about abandoning it. There are too many people like him."

Flynn reached across the table and took her hands. "I'm sorry, Tessa. I can't imagine how hard this is to hear. But I really believe we have a chance to figure out how to stop them and keep you safe if we pool all our resources."

All? "You're thinking more than just you and me, aren't you?"

Flynn nodded. "If you agree. I think the Midnight Security team could help us. They're reliable, trustworthy people. Tansy's brother Joe and foster-brother Nico are two of the best agents in the FBI. Sam was up there with them before he left. We're surrounded by some really smart people."

So many people who would know her business. "And they'd all be in danger because of me. They'd all become potential targets."

"I think it's a risk they'd be willing to take. These are your friends, Tessa. They'll want to help."

Panic galloped through her veins. She hadn't known them that long. How could she ask them to face this with her? "I don't know, Flynn. I don't know if I can take the risk."

His deep brown eyes warmed. "Your call, Tessa. I'm behind you no matter what you want. Let's go through the rest of what I know and then make some decisions. Or at least get a good night's sleep."

Tessa wanted to turn and look at the bed behind her, wanted to drag Flynn over to it and take another step forward with him. If she did that and then had to go into hiding again, would she survive the heartbreak? Or would the risk be worth it?

As if he was reading her mind, Flynn's eyes heated and he grinned. "Put on your problem solving hat, Tessa. We've got a lot of work to do before we can get to the fun stuff."

Her skin flushed and she had to look away. "Then let's work."

Even Flynn's chuckle was sexy. But his words became brisk and matter-of-fact as he described the evidence surrounding her family. Gambling. Money laundering. And worse, horrific stories of women and children being trafficked to other countries. Years of circumstantial evidence, but not enough to prove her grandfather's connection to any of it or to bring him to trial. Not when there were bigger problems to worry about.

Flynn tapped his pen on his notebook. "I keep going back to the night of the explosion and the number of people in the house."

It bothered her too, but it was still difficult to go back and remember that horrible day.

"I think we should assume the man in the room with you was killed." Flynn's voice was harder than it had been. "And I can't say I'm sorry about that. He deserved exactly what he got."

Tessa nodded. She felt the same.

"Do you know how many explosions you heard?"

She'd gone over it so many times in her head. "At least six. Unless the concussion I had messed with my hearing. But I heard four or five before the one near the room blew. And then I don't remember any more."

Flynn moved his chair around the table and sat beside her. His big arm wrapped her in a side hug. "I'm sorry to make you go back. I want to see if your memory matches the police or FBI reports."

"Do those match up?"

He kissed her forehead. "Smart girl. No, they don't. At least, they're not identical. The FBI report is much more detailed than the one produced by the local Sheriff's department. It has information that was never released to the press."

"Still only two deaths reported?"

He sighed and hugged her. "Three. The two male remains and you."

That was a horrid thing to hear. An official report of her death. "Why wouldn't they have told the truth in the report? And if they lied about my death, did they lie about anything else? Everything else?"

Flynn's hand ran up and down her arm. "As I said, smart girl. Until yesterday, I believed the report was accurate, although I wasn't sure of the identities of the two men. I'm sure people with more clearance than I have know the truth, but to keep witnesses safe, FBI reports don't include all the details."

That made sense, but it still made it creepy. Her death was in an official report.

She finally asked the question that had been circling in her head. "Do you think my father and my uncle are dead, or do you think they've been in hiding with the Pavic family all this time?"

Flynn sighed. "I don't know. I always thought it was a weird way to kill people. Even as a kid. There have to be easier ways to take out a person than blowing up a large house."

"Did the report say how many explosions?"

"Twelve."

"Twelve?" There must have been nothing left. Which wasn't a loss. It was only a house, not a home.

"How good are you at sketching people?"

Flynn's question had her sitting back and looking at him. "I draw a mean stick person. Why?"

He smiled. "I was hoping you could draw the men you'd seen that night. And your father and uncle. There aren't any photos of them. There are files of known associates of the Pavic family, identified and unidentified. If you could draw, then I could compare them at work. I can't access the files outside of the buildings and we're not taking you into an FBI office."

Even with the blows to the head and the concussion, she was pretty sure she could describe the other men, especially the one who'd wanted to rape her. "I can maybe describe them to someone. If you have someone you trust."

He hugged her again. "I think I know just the person."

F lynn rolled the idea around in his head for a bit. It would definitely mean letting more people know Tessa had a different bio than her Wit Sec one. Was it worth the risk?

Tessa tilted her head to look up. "Who is it? Can they be trusted?"

"Her name is Josie Ellis. She's an artist from Sacramento who volunteers her time to do police sketches. She's worked a lot with Nico Rivera. I've only met her a few times, but I'd say she can be trusted. Probably best to check in with Nico, though."

Tessa's body tightened against his. "Every time the circle gets bigger, I worry about putting these people in danger. I can't ask a random stranger to put herself at risk by helping me. No."

Her answer was frustrating, but he understood, even if he didn't agree. "We'll figure it out."

Tessa tapped her fingers on the table. "There must be computer apps out there that do that kind of thing. Once we're back at the lodge, I can try some. I'd also like to see the data you've collected over the years. Maybe I can find some patterns."

Flynn knew Tessa had helped Mitch and Bella solve the case of a serial arsonist. She'd been recruited by the FBI for her skills as a data analyst. Knowing her passion for and understanding of numbers, none of it surprised him.

"Did your father ever talk about where he traveled? Anything about associates?"

"We really didn't speak often and we never had casual conversations."

God. What a life. Even though he wasn't on the ranch, he talked with his parents and his brothers several times a week. She'd been in the same house with the man and they'd rarely spoken.

"Maybe something in my notes will trigger something."

She nodded then stood up. "Let's head back to the lodge. I'd like to see your data, see if I can find anything. Otherwise I'm going to have to call John and make new plans."

Panic raced through him. "Not yet. We haven't even had a day to work on this. We need to give it a real effort before you try to disappear."

She gave him a sad smile. "Try? I've managed it effectively for over a decade. The Marshals know what they're doing."

"I know. But this time, I know you're alive. And this time, I'm not letting you disappear from my life."

Her eyes filled with tears and she kissed him softly on the lips. "I don't want to disappear, but if it'll keep others safe, you know I'll have to go."

"Not alone. Not this time."

She shook her head. "No way. You're not leaving your family behind. You're too important to each other." Her back was stiff as she glared at him.

He kept her hand in his as he stood. "It wouldn't be forever. Just to give us enough time to figure things out."

When she started to speak, he stopped her with a quick kiss. "Let's not argue about it now. We're not at decision time yet. Let's give it another twenty-four hours and see where we're at."

Tessa stared into his eyes, not giving him any idea as to her thought process. Finally, she nodded. "Fine. Unless something changes. If I think I'm putting anyone in danger, I won't stay."

Knowing that was as good as he was going to get, he nodded back.

He also knew she wasn't going to get a chance to go anywhere without him.

CHAPTER 10
Second Set Of Hands

Tessa experienced a serious case of déjà vu as they paddled back to the lodge. The sun was behind the mountains and the night was cool. Two silhouettes awaited her on the dock. The big difference was that this time, Flynn was in the canoe with her.

Nerves skittered through her at the sight of those silhouettes, making her wonder if they should turn around. Surely someone from the lodge would have called them if there was trouble, if someone had arrived looking for her.

Flynn's soft voice reached her. "Relax. It's Sam and Tansy."

He read her fear so easily. For the past decade, she'd worked hard to contain her emotions and to ensure that no one saw her nerves. All the progress she'd made had disappeared with Flynn's reappearance. Her blank facade wasn't her automatic default state anymore. She needed that back. She needed to squash the emotions rolling through her.

And the desires. Flynn had awakened them all. She wanted a normal life, with a future filled with love and family. She'd trained herself not to want those, not to think about the future in personal terms. How was she supposed to go back to that?

Sam's silhouette waved and Tessa forced down the nerves and

reached for everything in her that was Tessa. When the canoe bumped softly against the dock, Sam reached down for her to hand him the rope.

Tansy spoke softly. "You got Ginger to come with you. That's amazing. Want me to take her while you get out?"

Tessa passed the cat up and Ginger let out a yowl that had them all smiling.

Tansy grinned. "Looks like she doesn't quite trust everyone yet."

Flynn had already jumped up to the dock and he reached down to help Tessa up. It reminded her that if she had to make a run for it, then she needed a better plan than actually running. Her weakness would cost her everything if it came to an actual race. Her job would be to make sure it didn't cost anyone else a single thing.

When she was standing on the dock, Tansy passed her the squirming cat. Ginger immediately settled into her arms. "It's amazing what a little food can do. I'm thinking she'll attach herself to everyone who feeds her."

Jetson nuzzled Sam and Tansy for pets as if he'd been absent for days.

These humans. These animals. The love that surrounded them. All of it made Tessa's throat tighten. She wanted to stay with these people in this amazing environment.

She didn't want to run and hide. She wanted to stay and fight. But what right did she have to ask any of them to take the chance that she could bring danger into their midst?

Jetson returned to her side and Flynn's arm came around her shoulder.

Tansy touched her arm. "Tessa? Are you okay? Can you tell us what's happening? We can help. We want to help."

She looked from one concerned face to the next and finally nodded. "Maybe. I'm not sure yet, but maybe. I think I'm ready to talk about it."

Flynn squeezed her shoulder and the others nodded.

Sam pointed to the side. "Why don't we use the Midnight Security Office? Tansy's creating a magic shield that prevents eavesdropping."

Tansy rolled her eyes. "It's not magic and it's not a shield. And we don't even know if it works in all circumstances yet. Or how big of an area..."

Sam cut off her words with a kiss. "Magic. And you can consider this a test."

Tansy laughed. "It'll take me a minute or two to set up."

While Tansy did her thing, Sam showed Flynn around the office. That caused her to feel more guilt. Because he'd spent most of his time since arriving with her, he hadn't even checked out the business he owned with his partners.

And now she was going to ask more of him and the others. Ginger leapt off her lap to explore the new space, but Jetson came over to nuzzle her hands before he settled at her side.

When Tansy said she was ready, the men returned to the table. Flynn sat beside her and took her hand. Tansy and Sam sat opposite them.

They all looked at her.

Her words blurted out before she could stop them. "I'm sorry. My life is a disaster and I may be bringing danger to you and your place. I may have already done so."

Tansy reached across the table and held out her hand until Tessa put hers in it. Tansy's eyes were steady on hers. "You would never deliberately target us. We know you. We like you. We trust you. Whatever this mess is, please let us help you straighten it out. We want to help."

Were her tears ever going to dry up? Tessa closed her eyes until she'd battled them back. When she opened them, she smiled at Tansy. "Thank you, but you need to reserve judgment on that until you hear as much of the story as I can tell you."

"It won't change our minds, but we'll listen."

Tessa nodded. "Okay. As I think you know, I'm in Wit Sec. Have been since high school when Flynn and I were friends."

She drew in a deep breath, tried to keep it succinct. "My mother died when I was a baby and I lived with my father, but didn't have a real relationship with him. I was told to stay in my room whenever there were others in the house. My father was apparently into criminal activities like gambling, money laundering, drugs, and more."

Flynn squeezed her hand and she looked down at the table to force out the next bit. "One day, my uncle set me up and convinced my father I was ratting him out, even though I knew absolutely nothing about his business. I was beaten and locked up. The house blew up and I was in a coma for a while. When I woke up, I required some surgeries and was kept away from the internet until I'd regained my physical abilities. I've been in Wit Sec ever since."

Her voice started to shake, so she took in a deep breath and continued. "Flynn has been looking into the crime family associated with my father and uncle. They were reported dead in the explosion, but so was I. We don't know if they're alive. I assume the family knows Flynn is investigating and that they keep tabs on him. If they follow him here and see me, it could go bad quickly. I don't want any of you hurt because of me."

But she didn't want to leave, and that made her incredibly selfish.

Tansy and Sam exchanged glances. She could see love and understanding in that quick exchange.

They turned back to her and Sam leaned his elbows on the table. "Sounds like we need a plan. Actually, it sounds like we need a couple of plans. One for if we wait to see if someone shows up. Another for if we want to take a more proactive approach and eliminate the threat before it arrives."

She waited for the third option, for her to leave. It didn't come.

Instead, Tansy spoke. "I can't imagine what you've been through, Tess. Your family isn't what real families are like." Tansy's eyes misted. "I've been lucky. I had an amazing family growing up. When my parents were killed, I lucked into a second amazing family. And now we're making another family with all of you here. We're going to help you. We're going to find a way. That's what family does."

Tears slipped down her cheeks and she had to squeeze her lips to keep in the sob.

That's what family does.

And they considered her one of the family.

Flynn knew Tessa was completely overwhelmed by Tansy's words. He also knew she didn't want to cry again. He squeezed her hand and kissed her hair.

"Told you so, Contessa."

That made her smile and she wiped her cheeks dry. "Thank you, everyone. I don't really know what to say. And I don't want anyone to get hurt."

Sam rose and walked around the table. He kissed Tessa's hair and patted her shoulder as he walked by and put a kettle on the stove. "Tansy prefers the peach ginger tea for evening planning. Would you like that or do you have a different preference? It's all caffeine free so you'll be able to sleep."

Tessa snorted. "That might require a miracle."

Sam grinned. "Then you've come to the right place. Miracles are Tansy's specialty. Flynn, if you want to grab a laptop, there are a few on the desks upstairs."

Flynn nodded and jogged up to check out the loft office he'd heard about. The setup was efficient and used the space well. Four desks and a table for group conversations. Just seeing the space had him wanting to dive into the company right away.

But he had work to do before that happened. He grabbed a laptop and headed down. He powered it up and looked at the group. "I can't access the FBI files from here, but I've got a lot of the information duplicated in my own files."

Sam had him hook his laptop up to the projector so they could all see the data on the big screen in the room.

"I've collected the data into various files. One for each of the major players. Grigor Pavic, the head of the family. His son Karlo. Martin Blanco, who is Tessa's father. Karlo and Martin are the two who were presumed dead in the house explosion that sent Tessa into Wit Sec."

He pulled up more files. "I have lists of crimes in what they consider their territory, which is mostly in the northwest area in and around Houston, along with some port connections down on the Gulf."

He'd divided the files by type of criminal activity. Gambling, money laundering, prostitution, drugs, human trafficking. Flynn smiled at Tessa. "I even started to like spreadsheets." She smiled softly at him, probably remembering his aversion to them in high school.

He pulled up his main one. "This isn't my forte, but I've listed as much information per crime as I could find." Type of crime, date, people involved, dollar value, victims, snitches, area, officers involved.

He scrolled down the sheet, letting them see the extent of crimes he suspected were connected to Pavic.

Tessa sighed. "And this is considered an insignificant organization in the grand scheme of criminal organizations?"

Flynn nodded. "Sadly. There are hundreds of larger groups involved in this kind of thing, dozens in the Houston area alone. I think Pavic knows if he stays small, he can remain off the major radars."

Sam nodded. "Getting greedier is what takes down a lot of criminals. If Pavic keeps to his status quo, there are always worse people out there for law enforcement to worry about."

Tansy's eyes were wide. "Worse than this? What is wrong with people?"

Sam pulled her in for a hug. "Poverty. Greed. Narcissism. Desire for power. Lack of empathy. Horrible childhoods. And some are just pure evil."

The big man kissed her hair and squeezed her. "But there are more good people in the world. More people who are making things better, fighting the evil, and looking out for each other."

Flynn saw tears sparkling in Tessa's eyes again, but she blinked them away.

When she spoke, her eyes stayed on his. "So, we need a plan for our group of good guys to prevent this particular group of assholes from doing any more damage."

"That's exactly it."

She nodded and looked at Sam. "Is there another laptop I can use to start collating my own data?"

While Sam went to grab one from the loft, Tansy looked at Flynn. "Do you have any photos of the people involved? Any photos of groups of them to see body language and connections? Anyone who could possibly be one of the men who were supposedly killed in the explosion?"

"Not many, but I'll pull up what I have. There are more in the FBI files, but still not many. There are no official photos of Martin or Karlo."

Tansy tapped her fingers on the table. "If they're involved in gambling, casino footage should show something. As long as they're using public casinos, which I assume they would to launder their money. But if we have pictures of who we're looking for, we might be able to tap into other data."

Flynn grinned at Tansy. "I thought you were a physicist and inventor, not an FBI agent."

She rolled her eyes but smiled. "It's all puzzles, patterns and problem solving, right Tessa?"

Tessa nodded but didn't smile. She looked at Flynn as Sam handed her another laptop. "If you had pictures of the faces, would it really help gather data?"

"It would." He knew she was thinking of their earlier conversation about the sketch artist.

Sam nodded. "We use facial recognition software all the time in the FBI. If the social media sites can search and tag people from their personal posts, imagine what the government's software can find. That's how they track down a lot of known associates, find boltholes and vehicles."

Tessa's worried gaze turned back to Flynn. "I don't think it's worth the risk."

Sam frowned. "What isn't?"

Tessa sighed. "Flynn suggested I work with a sketch artist to create images of my father, uncle, and the other men in the house that day."

Sam nodded. "That's a good idea. What about Josie?"

Flynn hated the defeat on Tessa's face. "Tessa is worried about bringing anyone else into our little circle. She's afraid that they'll become targets as well."

Tansy reached for Tessa's hand again. "I know the feeling. It's really hard putting your trust and your faith in people when it means potentially putting them in danger as well. But these people are the best at what they do. If we all work as a team, we're pretty unstoppable."

Sam joined in. "You two ladies are pretty much the smartest people I know. We can figure out a way to do this and keep everyone safe."

Tessa didn't look entirely convinced.

Flynn scrambled for an idea. "What if we had some kind of party or event where it would seem natural for extra people to come in? Then we could add in Joe and Nico along with Josie."

Sam agreed. "We could do something with Midnight Security. Run a training course maybe. This weekend is free for everyone. We've got three days open. We'll need to loop in the others and get them here soon."

Tansy nodded. "We've got Marcus and Troy in town who would jump right in to help as well. Others too."

Tessa shook her head and shoved to her feet. "It's too much. Too much danger for everyone. I can't put so many people at risk. I'm sorry. I can't do it."

Tansy and Sam both protested, but she kept shaking her head and backing away.

Flynn shoved to his feet, but she kept moving away. "We'll figure it out, Tessa. Give us a chance, here."

"I'm sorry. It's too dangerous for you. For all of you. I can't do it."

And she walked out the door.

CHAPTER 11
Second Wind

Panic clawed at Tessa's throat but it wasn't for her. It was for these amazing people around her. She couldn't bring the threat of danger to their doorstep. She couldn't risk Tansy's new family.

After years of tamping down her emotions and keeping them under control, they were swamping her. Waves of hope, fear, determination, panic, desire, and love kept slamming into her.

She heard Flynn call her name softly but she kept moving. It wasn't like he couldn't catch her. He wouldn't even need to jog if she moved at her top speed. Which she wasn't.

Then his big, strong body was in front of her and he said her name softly again. He draped her coat around her shoulders and then his arms wrapped around her and he drenched her with his warmth.

They stood there for long minutes, not saying a thing, with his heat slowing her shaking and filling her heart. "I'm so scared, Flynn."

He kept holding her, kept making her feel not only safe but wanted. "I know, honey. I know."

"I don't want you to get hurt. Any of you."

He chuckled and kissed her hair. "Feeling's mutual."

"Hiding is so much easier than fighting."

A larger chuckle rumbled through him. "But it's not as much fun."

She leaned back to look up at him. "Fun?"

He smiled. "I'm standing in the moonlight with a strong and sexy woman wrapped in my arms. Fun."

She shook her head but had to smile, too. "Men."

"We've got your back, Tessa. All of us. And we have skills. Again, all of us. We need *your* skills to help us collate the data into something useful, something we can use. Then we can form a plan of action. Until then, we keep life going as normal here. No one knows you're here. And no one's able to just drop in and take your photo. You're safe. We're safe. And we'll all be safer if we can eliminate the threat."

She tucked herself back into his hug while she thought about his words. They made sense. They were logical. Was it her heart making her think that? Was she selfishly staying?

"Come on. I told the others we'd talk again in the morning. Let's get some rest. It's always easier to think clearly when we're not exhausted."

She nodded and Flynn kept her under his arm as they moved into the lodge.

As they opened the door, she remembered the cat. "I forgot Ginger."

As if the thought had conjured them up, Sam and Tansy walked up behind them with the cat. Jetson followed. Tansy smiled as the cat leapt from her arms and moved to explore the space. "I've been researching natural cat litters. I've got Aisling bringing some sawdust up from the sawmill for tonight. But there are good options with corn, wheat, pine, grass seeds. It'll be fun to try the different options and see which are most effective."

Sam rolled his eyes. "Only you would think litter box experiments might be fun."

They all laughed, but Tessa turned to them. "I'm sorry I walked out. I'm a little overwhelmed."

Tansy smiled. "And tired and scared and worried. No problem. Why don't we talk again in the morning? The guys don't have clients coming until ten, so there's lots of time. And there's no rush."

Sam nodded. "You know we've got a lot of safety precautions in place. We'll have lots of warning if a problem comes to us."

They weren't upset with her and still wanted to help. Tessa hugged them both and then headed up the stairs to her room with Flynn on her heels.

He leaned against the door frame and smiled. "Why don't I grab us something to eat? Then we can get some actual sleep. We're all safe here."

Her stomach growled, but the thought of climbing down and back up the stairs while she was so tired wasn't a fun one. She smiled. "Sounds good. I think I'll grab a shower, but I'll be quick."

Flynn's eyes heated and she wanted to invite him to join her in the shower. But she wasn't quite that brave.

He grinned. "Go ahead. That thought will give me some fantasies to enjoy later tonight. I'll be back in a few."

This time, it wasn't fear or panic that had her heart pounding. It was pure desire. She'd been too broken for too long to give much thought to sex, but when Flynn had reappeared in her life, he'd woken that part of her.

She wanted him. Wanted to explore a whole new world with him. But that would mean he'd see all the scars, find all the ways in which she'd been broken.

As she bundled her hair on top of her head and moved into the shower, she tried to look herself over with a critical eye. Scars crisscrossed her legs and wrists. There were more on her sides where they'd had to fix ribs and lungs. Then the burn scars on her back.

Overall, she was a mess.

She'd always wanted to get tiny flowers tattooed into the web of scars. All the flowers Flynn's dad had mentioned. Including one for the mother she'd never known. A rose for Rosa. But sitting in a tattoo shop for the required hours was too big a risk. She'd been told to blend in. Fade into the background. Don't have anything stand out that could identify her.

If Flynn's idea worked, she could take the risk. Get the tattoos she wanted. The ones that would remind her of the good things and people in life.

Tessa quickly dried off and threw on the yoga pants and t-shirt she'd brought in with her. Her body was tingling and she wondered what Flynn would do if she walked out in a towel. Or naked.

She wanted to be that brave, wanted to take that step. But she was also working mostly on adrenaline. Maybe after she had a few hours' sleep, she could make better sense of everything.

She wasn't going to use Flynn to block out the fear. If she slept with him, it would be because she was clear-headed enough to know she was ready to take that step.

Tessa dumped her clothes in the hamper and realized it was full enough for Tansy's latest CleanySaurs to do laundry for her in the morning. May ran the machines while Tag was programmed to sort and fold.

Mind-boggling.

A soft knock on the door had her jumping. Her nerves were frayed with all the thoughts about sex.

"Just me." Flynn, of course.

Tessa opened the door to his lopsided grin, which had her thoughts skittering back to sex.

"Room service."

She smiled and gestured with a flourish for him to come in.

Flynn set the tray down on the desk Aisling had made. Tessa realized the chair in front of the desk was the only seat in the room. Other than the bed. Her gaze tracked from the chair to the bed and back, then she looked up at Flynn.

His eyes were dark and twinkling with fun. "I'll be right back."

She hadn't moved an inch when he returned moments later, dressed in flannel pants and a soft grey t-shirt that hugged his muscular frame. Was she drooling?

He waved a tablet in his hand. "How about we sit on the bed and zone out to a movie?"

She nodded slowly, not quite able to verbalize. He wasn't wearing socks or shoes and something about his bare feet felt intimate.

She was losing her mind.

Flynn angled the tablet to show her a fun superhero movie. "This one good?"

She nodded but flinched when he took her hand. His grin was sexy and had her heart racing. "Relax, Tessa. I'm not going to jump you."

She shook her head at her ridiculous thoughts and clambered onto the bed, hoping she would regain her power of speech soon.

Flynn moved the tray to the side table and used a pillow to prop up the tablet, then passed her a bowl of soup that smelled like heaven. They sat shoulder to shoulder and he used his toe to start the movie, making her laugh again.

His growly voice had her shivering before his words registered. "Unless you ask."

It took her a moment to place his words in context of his previous statement.

He wasn't going to jump her.

Unless she asked.

Flynn loved the flush on Tessa's skin whenever he teased her. Her life had been so serious. It was nice to be able to give her moments of light and fun. And if that light and fun took a sexy turn, even better.

They were both on edge with all the sexual tension humming between them. He wouldn't push at all, but it was fun to play around. A way to help her forget the crap that filled her life. He leaned into her shoulder gently. Not enough to be obnoxious, but enough to remind her she wasn't alone.

They downed the soup and then the cheese and homemade crackers he'd found. When they were finished, he put all the plates on the tray and then moved back onto the bed. He held up his arm and Tessa snuggled right in.

It felt exactly right.

He ran his hand up and down her arm gently. Played with her curls. Enjoyed the feel of her body curled safely beside his. As they relaxed, Flynn let his mind wander. It was often the key to finding answers. If he focused too hard, things remained elusive. When he gave his brain time to rove, it sometimes helped data coalesce.

If he had a horse here, he'd go for a ride, give the horse its head and just go. Of course, the thick forests and hilly countryside of Vermont might not be the best ride. Or maybe it would. He'd have to check into that.

Slowly, Tessa's breathing relaxed and her body softened. She drifted into sleep and blew Flynn away with her trust that she would be safe with him. Even with the attraction zipping between them, she trusted him to not take advantage of her. Lack of sleep on the previous night had his own eyes closing and he let himself drift off.

Hours later, Tessa woke him when she let out a cry of pain. The soft nightlight she had in her room allowed him to see that she was still asleep. Her face was contorted with pain and she let out another gasp.

She was still under his arm, so he wrapped her more tightly and whispered. "It's okay, Tessa. You're safe. I'm here. I've got you."

A whimper escaped her but she turned into his chest and gripped his shirt. He repeated the words and held her firmly while her body shuddered and she muffled her pain against his chest.

She might as well have reached into his ribcage and punched his heart. The pain was as real.

Sure, he'd realized fairly quickly he was being a jackass when he was pissed at her for hiding from him. He'd finally looked at the situation from her perspective.

But hearing her in such pain, whether it was real or memory, hit him hard. She'd lived a loveless childhood and then had her life ripped away in high school. Her body had been broken in too many ways to count.

But she was alive. She'd thrived in her new life. She'd found a job she enjoyed and a circle of friends. No way in hell was he letting anyone take that from her again. She'd more than earned the second chance at a full life.

He wanted to ease the pain from her and drop it in the bodies of the men who'd caused it. Was her father alive? Was he the one who had set the explosion? Someone else in the Pavic family or a rival?

His gut told him it was some kind of scheme created by the uncle to either get himself and his brother off the law enforcement radar, or a way to eliminate Tessa's father.

He'd remained open to all possibilities over the years, but there had been no one to gain financially from the death of Martin and Karlo. Except the family.

Tessa sighed softly and her hand opened and relaxed on his chest. Her breathing told him she'd drifted into a deeper sleep and he closed his own eyes.

The dogs barking outside woke them both several hours later. Flynn jumped up and rushed to the window, only to spot the dogs playing in the newly fallen snow.

Heart racing, he turned to grin at a wide-eyed Tessa. "Looks like we got a few inches of snow last night. The dogs are having a blast."

She thumped back down to the bed and blew out a breath.

Flynn slipped back in with her and pulled her into his arms. He could feel her heart pounding where she snuggled up against him. "How'd you sleep?"

Tessa laughed softly. "Best sleep in as long as I can remember. I should have warned you about my nightmares. Did I disturb you?"

He kissed her hair and squeezed. "I slept great, too."

She sighed. "Which means I did have the nightmares. I'm sorry I woke you up. I'm glad they weren't too bad."

That wasn't too bad? "What happens during a bad night?"

She shook her head. "Think panic attack combined with terrified toddler. It's not pretty. That's why I took the room farthest from everyone else."

"I'm sorry you have to live with those."

She shrugged then stacked her hands on hands on his chest and rested her chin on top. "Thank you."

Flynn raised his eyebrows. "For what?"

She smiled. "For being a great guy. For holding me through the dreams. For treating me like I'm normal and not screwed up beyond repair."

He rolled them over so he was on top of her, but he braced his weight on his forearms. "You're not beyond repair. You're whole and healthy. You've been through hell and you've grown into this amazing woman who takes care of others and the planet. A woman who is kind and generous. A gorgeous woman inside and out."

He watched Tessa's eyes widen as he spoke and then saw the smile begin deep inside and grow until her face caught up.

"Thank you." Her whispered words were full of emotion, but she maintained eye contact. "You're a pretty special guy, Flynn Walker."

When he rolled his eyes, she leaned up to kiss his jaw.

"In fact, I think you're special enough to do me a favor."

"Anything you need."

Her eyes lit up and her smile broadened. "That's exactly what I wanted to hear."

This time, she kissed him lightly on the lips. "Okay, Cowboy. I need your help with a pretty big step. A step I'm one hundred percent certain I want to take."

Flynn tried to control his body's reaction to her words in case she wasn't saying what he thought she was saying.

The sparkle in her eyes had him hoping.

"I want you to be my first, Flynn. Make love to me."

Hell, yeah.

CHAPTER 12

Ladies First

Tessa knew she was being bold and risking rejection, but she couldn't hold back her words or her desire. Flynn had always been the best man she knew. She'd been in love with him almost since sitting beside him in math class.

He'd proven himself time and again. And she wanted it all. Her life was precarious. She wanted to experience everything Flynn was willing to give her.

At her words, Flynn's eyes darkened and his hold tightened. "Are you sure? Really sure?"

She nodded. "I'm sure. If you are. If you're not ready to take that step, I completely understand."

The lopsided grin she loved so much kicked up. He let more of his weight settle onto her so there was no mistaking that his body was on board.

Then his mouth crashed onto hers. The kiss was all tongue and teeth and fire. So much fire. It wouldn't have surprised her if their sleepwear simply poofed into flames.

When Flynn pulled back so they could breathe, he trailed kisses along her jawline and to her earlobe. He nipped, then soothed the area with his tongue while she tried to control the shivers covering her.

Flynn's hands scooted under her t-shirt and feathered up her torso until they brushed against her breasts.

He leaned back enough to see her face. "Okay?"

She loved that he asked, but she wanted to lose herself in the moment, not stop and have to rethink again and again.

"More than okay. Touch. Touch everything. In every way. With all the parts of you."

He grinned and kissed her hard and quick. "That sounds perfect. But if you change your mind or want to slow down, all you have to do is say so. It's your call. Always."

Her heart melted a little bit more. "Got it. Appreciate it. Now, kiss me again."

He grinned and devoured her mouth again. And again.

When his hands moved, his touch was exquisite. Tender. Enticing. Intoxicating.

Her brain was filled only with bubbles of desire when Flynn growled and sat up. "Too many clothes. I want to taste you."

He yanked his own shirt over his head and tossed it, then eased hers up and did the same. She was too busy admiring him to think of anything else.

And then his mouth covered her breast and thinking became overrated.

Her body had felt attraction before, but this was on a whole new level. She'd never known her body could respond in this way.

She breathed out his name and he chuckled against her skin. "We're just getting started, darling. Hang on to something because I've got a lot of exploring to do."

He slowly drifted down her body and when he reached her yoga pants, he dipped his fingers beneath the hem.

She wanted them to melt away, wanted his mouth touching her in the most intimate of ways.

"Getting there, honey, but there's no need to rush." His smug response told her that she'd spoken aloud. She was losing her mind in pleasure because the man was turning out to be a master explorer.

And she'd never felt better.

Flynn eased the yoga pants and panties down, kissing along the exposed skin.

She knew she should be worrying about his reaction to her scars. She knew she should be hiding herself away.

But she wasn't and she didn't.

This was Flynn and he kissed her skin as if he relished it all. As if all of her skin was beautiful and scar free.

Her eyes filled with tears at the beauty of that thought. He didn't care she'd been broken. Didn't care that she had the scars to prove it.

When he slid her clothing off her feet, he sat back on his haunches and smiled. His gaze roved from one area to the next, and his smile only grew. "You are a gorgeous woman, Tessa. Now, let's get back to business."

He picked up her foot and kissed her ankle. He moved up her leg as slowly as he'd descended. By the time he reached her knee, she was quivering with need.

As he moved up her thighs, he started talking. Soft murmurs that filled her up and had the desire almost ready to burst.

You're beautiful.

So strong

Smart and sexy.

Smell like heaven.

Perfect.

None of those things were true, but when he said them, she believed.

Then the words turned dirty.

She was surprised to find herself spiraling higher the more he growled, the more he described exactly what he wanted to do with her.

He used his hands to gently widen her legs, and then he grinned at her wickedly. "Hang on."

His tongue swiped along her seam and then dipped inside. If his hand hadn't been holding down her hip, she would have shot right off the bed.

He chuckled and the reverberations in that most intimate of places had her gasping out his name.

"You're amazing, Tessa. Let's see that first orgasm." Then his tongue went to work and he slid a finger inside.

With a noise she couldn't identify coming out of her own throat, Tessa arched off the bed as the power bolted through her. Everything inside her burst and shivered as wave after wave of sensation filled her.

Flynn's mouth and fingers continued to work their magic and when she had enough energy to open her eyes, she found his gaze locked on hers. "So damn gorgeous. That was the sexiest thing I've ever seen."

She wanted to respond, wanted to tell him to grab a condom, but speech was still beyond her.

His smile was cocky, but she wasn't about to complain. He'd earned it.

"Round two, Tessa. Let's get you reaching even higher."

F lynn watched Tessa float through her second orgasm.

His own body was rock hard and desperate for action, but he wanted to make sure she was ready. He'd never been with a virgin before and he wanted to make sure the experience was as good for her as he could make it.

How could no one have realized what a gorgeous woman she was inside and out? He wanted her to know it, feel it, believe it.

This time when Tessa's eyes opened, they were glazed but she smiled at him. He crawled up her body and kissed her lightly. "Hey."

"Hey. Wow." She blinked a few times. "Hey."

He smiled and kissed her again. "How you feeling?"

Her smile could have powered up all the solar panels on the property, and there were a lot of them.

"I'm feeling better than anyone has a right to feel. Better than I've ever felt before. But I'm also feeling like we haven't quite got to the good part yet."

"You want to keep going?"

She laughed. "More than anything else in the world right now. You have any condoms, Cowboy?"

Shit. Not here. He'd only worn his sleep pants and a t-shirt to her room.

Her eyes widened and her mouth dropped open. "You don't?"

"Not here. Across the hall. Twenty seconds away. Do not move. Not a muscle. Not one muscle."

He leapt off the bed and tossed the covers over her. When he reached the door, he pointed at her. "Not one muscle."

Flynn threw open the door and jumped into his room. He raced into the bathroom and grabbed his travel bag. He dumped the bag into the sink and snagged the condoms he had in there.

Then he flew back across the hall, closed the door, threw the lock, and held up the strip of condoms in his hand. "Success."

Tessa laughed and sat up, letting the blanket slip to her waist. She crooked her finger.

He took two steps but then she held up her finger and he froze. Had she changed her mind? The twinkle in her eye said differently.

She pointed at his flannel pants and then swung the finger up and down, indicating he needed to take them off.

"Gladly."

He shucked the pants without breaking eye contact with her. Her eyes strayed down his body and she smiled again.

Flynn found himself standing straighter, puffing up every muscle under her scrutiny. The woman made him feel like Superman.

When her gaze returned to his, she licked her lips and crooked her finger again.

He reached the end of the bed and crawled up her body until her mouth was within reach. Her arms came around his shoulders, but he didn't touch her with anything other than his mouth. It was the only way to hang onto his self-control.

Tessa ran her fingers through his hair then over his back, his shoulders, his biceps. Each feathery touch tested his will.

He wanted to pound into her and claim her as his. He wanted to shout from the rooftops that this amazing woman wanted him. And he wanted to go so slowly, so it would send her over the edge time and again before they were finished.

"Now, Flynn. Now."

Her whispered demand had him grinning as he leaned on one elbow and reached down to touch her again. He assumed it would be easier for her if she was as aroused as possible.

Her whisper became a chant as he added another finger to the mix. Then he played with her clit and when her body started to tighten, he slid on the condom and slipped inside her.

They both groaned at the same time and then smiled at each other.

Flynn kept his weight mostly off her as he slid out and then back in, each time a little deeper. He barely felt the resistance when he pushed through it, and Tessa gasped softly and closed her eyes.

He stopped moving and waited. It only took a few moments before her smile reappeared and those eyelashes lifted to reveal the smile reached deep.

"You good?" His voice was gruff.

She nodded. "It's already fading."

She reached up to kiss him, but he kept his body still and steady. The kiss built and then Tessa squeezed around him and he nearly lost his shit.

"I'm good Flynn, but I'll be better when you start moving."

He hoped so. Watching her closely, he stroked tentatively. Her mouth opened to let out a soft purr of pleasure. And she squeezed him again.

Holding onto his control had never been such a challenge.

If he hadn't been so intent on watching her reactions, his eyes might have rolled back in his head. She felt so damn good.

He changed the angle of his strokes, looking for the position that would bring her the most pleasure. When he hit it just right, Tessa let out another purr and whispered his name.

He wanted to hear that voice saying his name in exactly that tone every damn day for the rest of his life.

When she spiralled up and over the edge one final time, Flynn's control snapped.

He pounded into her, drawing out her orgasm as best as he could. When she cried out again, Flynn thrust three more times, then collapsed on her.

As he struggled to breathe and keep his weight off her, he wondered what the hell he would do if she disappeared on him again.

Because that would break him for good.

CHAPTER 13

Spur To Action

Tessa couldn't contain her smile. It was impossible to wipe it off her face. She was lucky she wasn't giggling uncontrollably. For so long, she hadn't thought she'd trust a man enough to sleep with him. But Flynn was different in the best of ways.

And sex with Flynn was far better than anything she'd read in her favorite romance novels. She'd scoffed at the feelings of elation described in the books. Now she felt them. She was living a moment that could be in a book.

A giggle escaped and Flynn raised his head with wide eyes. She laughed again but slammed a hand over her mouth.

"Giggling? I'm about dead from the best sex of my life and you're giggling?"

That had her laughing harder.

Flynn's lips twitched and then he grinned full on. "No need to ask if you're feeling okay?"

She shook her head and managed to reign in the laughter. "Sorry. I just never expected to feel so..." She waved her hand in an attempt to explain.

"So?"

"Good. Great. Relaxed and happy. I thought it would be uncomfortable and awkward but it was amazing." She leaned over and kissed him. "Thank you."

He barked out a laugh. "You're amazing, Tessa. And you're more than welcome."

Then he shook his head again, but kept smiling. "I should be the one thanking you. So, thank you for trusting me to be with you like this." His voice turned gruff and he swallowed hard. "Thank you."

Then he kissed her again, and the giggles slipped away under the tenderness of his kiss.

While their lips tangled, Flynn ran his hands over her body. Then he leaned up on his elbow and his gaze tracked where he touched her.

She realized he was experimenting with his touch, finding out where she reacted, where she didn't.

When their eyes locked again, he smiled. "Does me touching any of you hurt? Are any areas not responsive to touch?"

Tears welled at his gentle questions, but she swallowed hard. "Many of the nerve endings still work, but not all of them."

His hand didn't stop moving, didn't stop caressing. "Show me."

When she hesitated, he leaned in to kiss her. "I can tell a lot by how you react, but I don't want to hurt you or make you uncomfortable. Show me what areas you prefer me not to touch."

Love for this man filled her, filled the cracks. "They don't bother you?"

He rolled his eyes. "Only in the way that you shouldn't have had to suffer them in the first place. They're just scars and I've got plenty of my own."

That made her grimace. "I do remember a bull with a bad temper who did not appreciate you being on his back."

He grinned. "Didn't quite make the eight seconds on that one. Good old Zombullie. I think I've got a few from him."

"Did anyone ever manage to ride him?"

His grin turned cocky. "I did. Three times. In fact, the third successful ride at the National Finals was my last rodeo event. Figured rodeo didn't get better than beating Zombullie in the Finals."

She cupped his cheek. "I'm surprised you gave it up. You loved the adrenaline rush and the animals."

He smiled. "I did. But rodeo is a young man's game. I grew up."

In part because he'd thought she was dead and he wanted to find answers. She kissed him softly. "You grew up very well. I'm so proud of what you've accomplished, of what you do."

His skin flushed but he smiled and kissed her back. "I feel the same about you, Tessa. You're amazing. Now, stop distracting me and show me where it's not comfortable to be touched."

She blew out a breath and sat up. "Most of it is fine. The places where I've had multiple surgeries in the same spots are sometimes numb. Others can tingle and feel weird to touch. I avoid here."

It should have felt weird, sitting naked in bed and highlighting her scars, but Flynn made it seem like the most natural thing in the world.

He traced his fingers over the areas that didn't bother her and seemed to memorize the trouble spots. Instead of making her feel weak. It made her feel important. Cared for. Even loved. Although she was sure he wasn't thinking like that.

"I've wanted to get tattoos of flowers that would intertwine with the scars, make them look like vines." She hadn't expected to say that out loud.

"Sexy flower tattoos. I like it. Why haven't you done it?"

"I'm supposed to stay hidden, to fade away. Tattoos draw attention so they're off limits. The tattoo artist would have to see the scars and that would lead to questions. It's too risky."

Flynn's phone beeped, breaking the mood and reminding her they had a job to do if she was going to stay at Midnight Lake.

Flynn picked up his phone and sighed. "Sam has some time in about twenty minutes if we want to go over things at the Midnight Security cabin."

Tessa stretched her legs and started to shift. "That gives me enough time to shower and do some of my stretches."

Flynn held out a hand. "Sounds like a plan. I'd like to help with both."

Laughing, she let him help her up. He never made her feel less. Somehow, he made her feel stronger. Able to handle everything. And do it better with his help.

For the first time, maybe ever, she realized she truly wasn't alone.

Anger burned in Flynn's belly.

Tessa was strong in so many ways. She hadn't cried over her scars, although she'd been close when she'd checked over his. She understood the scars weren't ugly. They symbolized survival. Enhancing them with flowers and integrating that into her new name, her memories, and her being was important.

But the Pavic family made it impossible for her to do even that. It was time to take those bastards down.

They set up in the loft office of the Midnight Security cabin. That way if anyone came in the main door, they wouldn't see anything they shouldn't.

Sam and Graham had been the primary force behind the cabin's setup and it was perfect. On the main floor, the large room acted as a conference room with a long table and chairs, a whiteboard and screen. Up here, there were four desks clustered together and another screen.

At the moment, that screen showed the data from his files. Tessa sat at a desk with the laptop and she was scrolling through the data. She wore headphones and had told them she was listening to nature sounds as it helped her focus.

The speed with which she read and checked data was impressive. She'd always been an interested student and her ability to remember important information would be an asset to her in so many jobs. He was so glad she'd found one she enjoyed despite being unable to follow her Math-teacher dream.

When Tessa sat up straighter and scrolled more quickly, he and Sam stopped what they were doing and watched the screen where they'd projected her data.

She flipped back and forth between financial documents. Definitely not Flynn's forté. He tried to follow her thinking, but she changed screens too quickly for him to figure out what had caught her attention.

Sam frowned and looked over at Flynn. He shrugged back. He had no idea what she was seeing but her intense focus guaranteed she'd caught something important.

After a few minutes, she nodded her head, and took off her head-phones. She looked surprised to find both men watching her.

"What did you find?" The question slipped out before Flynn could stop it.

"Oh. I'm not a hundred percent sure, but there's a complex financial trail they've been trying to hide."

"How do you know they've been trying to hide it?"

She turned back to the laptop and scrolled through the screens, explaining as she went. When she was done, he looked at Sam, who was grinning while he shook his head. Flynn figured his friend had understood about the same as he had. Maybe half.

"Okay. Let's see how much of that I followed. There are fake companies and real companies and someone is using them all in a chain to hide money. And some of that money is landing in a personal account of someone you think is attached to Pavic. But that someone doesn't have a real identification."

Tessa smiled at them. "More or less. To have a bank account, debit or credit cards, you need to have identification. If you don't want those options, you need to have cash. And if you want cash that can't be labelled as dirty, you have to access it through a bank or some other institution."

Sam frowned. "And you've found someone linked to Pavic?"

"Maybe. I've found that a regular money trail goes into the account of Karl Kuzmetzov. Other than the information at the bank, there is zero record of a Karl Kuzmetzov anywhere. Well, not that I've found yet. I'd need more sophisticated programs to dig more."

Sam nodded. "I can send the name and information to Joe and Nico. Speaking of Joe and Nico, I want to bring them in on this. I know you're nervous Tessa, but they'd want to help. A bigger team means a bigger chance of success."

Flynn nodded, throwing his support behind his friend. He knew Tessa was worried about everyone else, but he was confident in the team of people he'd chosen to start a business with. He wanted her to trust them, too. Wanted her to trust him. Take a chance on them finding a solution. And giving them a chance at a future together.

Tessa looked from Sam to him and then simply stared into his eyes for a long moment. He took her hand and brushed his thumb over her wrist, avoiding the numb spot she'd pointed out.

Finally, she nodded. "Okay."

Sam mumbled a thanks and immediately started typing. Flynn was sure he was contacting their friends and getting them here as quickly as possible.

"Thank you." His quiet words had her smiling sadly.

He leaned over to kiss her, then leaned back. "Okay, Flower Girl, what's next?"

She smiled shakily at the comment and then pointed at her screen. "I want to try to get an overview of the financial structure of Pavic's organization. If I can see where the money flows with any kind of clarity, we should be able to find the blind spots. We may not know where they're hiding the money right away, but following the trail always gives us more information."

She took a breath and stared at the screen. "I also want to create a map. Seeing it laid out visually helps. A large map with markers for anything associated with Pavic. People, crimes, suspected crimes, targets, properties. That kind of thing."

Flynn nodded and stood. "That I can start on."

He moved back to his laptop and pulled up a map of Texas, then zoomed into Houston and the surrounding area. He could narrow it down by neighborhood but collect all the information on one giant map. Then Tessa could zoom in and out, looking for the connections.

Flynn was good with visual data. He had several smaller maps in his files already. Collating them all into one would be a big job, but not impossible. Seeing the entire area might help him as well.

Pavic didn't have a large area of control. There were more powerful gangs and groups out there. Flynn could use an overlay system to cover those territories. Then he could see where Pavic business overlapped with others.

Because her grandfather wasn't one of the major players, Pavic might get away with being involved with multiple gangs without pissing anyone off. He should have thought of this angle before.

A message beeped on his laptop from Sam. It showed the message he'd sent to Joe and Nico.

Rodeo King finally showed up to see Midnight Lake. How about we throw him a party? I bet Josie would love to come, too. How's Saturday?

Perfect. He grinned at Sam and nodded.

If he was a betting man, he'd say they'd have three new guests at the lodge soon. Despite being in high demand, or maybe because of that, Joe and Nico could take time off for important things. He'd bet they'd accumulated a ton of leave like he had.

And they were going to use it because Sam asked.

This was definitely a team he wanted to join full time. Once they'd locked up the threat against Tessa, he'd work to make sure she wanted him full-time as well.

CHAPTER 14

Second String

Tessa lost herself in the data. Her brain worked best when she read things over first in detail, then reread quickly while looking for connections. Flynn had collected a lot of data over the years and it was a time-consuming process.

This wasn't like the data she'd helped Bella sort and analyze. This was more like a spiderweb of information. Actually more like multiple spiderwebs intersecting.

The thought had her sitting back and imagining it. Three-dimensional spiderwebs intersecting at various points. Spherical spiderwebs. A three-dimensional Venn diagram gone mad.

What would be the most important points to ground the data? Places or individuals? Transactions? People made the most sense, so she'd start there.

She closed her eyes to help her envision the 3D webs. The first glowing point would be Grigor Pavic. His web would have the most threads, as he appeared to be at the center of the entire mess.

She'd need threads on his web for each branch of his organization. Legitimate casino interactions. Illegal gambling sites. Prostitution. Guns. Drugs. She didn't have information for all of those, but she'd rather have the possibilities in place so she could easily add in what she discovered. Those would be soft grey threads.

Green for finances. Those threads would criss-cross when the money moved between the branches of the Pavic organization. There would be many of those.

Once Grigor's web-sphere was cemented in her mind, she grabbed some paper and did a crude sketch. She might not be able to draw people, but she could make a sphere. Sort of. The result was something only a loving parent would post on the fridge, but it would help her to explain her thinking to others.

Now, who would warrant their own webs and who would be minor players who could be added to the various data points on the main webs?

Her gut was telling her that her Uncle Karlo had transformed himself into Karl Kuzmetzov. She'd put info on both personas on the same web. If they weren't the same person, she'd build another later.

Another for her father, although she hadn't come across any information that made her believe he was alive. She wasn't sure how she was supposed to feel about that. Gangs and organizations Pavic worked with would get their own spheres as well.

Any super-villain had a layer of sub-villains to run their empire. If her father or Uncle Karlo were still alive, that would likely be their positions. Hidden behind the scenes, running the money, conducting the orchestra of crimes.

Including the explosion of her house with her inside. With a deep breath, Tessa shoved aside the emotion. There was no place for it here.

She started creating the new web in her mind. The chain of dead-end transactions with no record of where the money landed. The date of the house explosion. From the very little she truly knew of her father and uncle, she figured the illegal gambling branch was the best fit for their personalities.

She could imagine one or both of them being in charge of illegal games. There were probably mobile ones that changed locations often, but from the data she'd been studying, she'd bet there was at least one permanent, well-hidden facility that held a private casino.

Where? This might be the key to finding them.

Tessa sketched out the second web-sphere, angling it so that the points of data would intersect with Grigor's.

As she added more spheres, the familiar excitement of being on the right track to solving a complex problem filled her. The illegal casino was the key. Once they located that, they would find the solutions to many of their questions.

Would the map Flynn was working on help? Maybe she and Flynn could collate the data together. Her heart fluttered at that thought. She wanted to do so much with him, but it might be too early to have real hope.

Tessa pulled off her headphones and gave herself a minute to switch from analysis to the real world. Her body was stiff, so she stretched her arms and shoulders, wiggled her fingers, and moved her neck. Next, she stood and stretched her back and finally moved her legs.

Flynn's drawl brought her back to the room. "Well, that's a sexy sight to greet a man."

She turned to the stairs where he'd appeared from below. "I thought you were working with Sam's class on outdoor tracking?"

He raised his eyebrows. "I was. We've been gone for over four hours."

She'd gotten lost in her data again. Knowing she was in a safe place had allowed her to sink into the information and not keep one eye on her surroundings.

The cabin had been locked and security cameras were trained on the door and windows. There would be lots of warning if someone tried to break in.

She'd been safe. A feeling she was getting used to.

Flynn walked over and kissed her. Another thing she was getting used to happening. Another thing she was craving and anticipating.

She didn't want to lose this. "I've got some ideas, but I need to check out that map we talked about. Have you had a chance to work on it yet?"

He grinned. "I did. And then I pulled in Bella. With her investigations on serial arsonists, she's good at working on maps."

Tessa had forced herself to stop panicking every time they brought another person into the group. She'd been on her own for most of her life, so it took some doing. But connecting with people was another thing she'd missed and now craved.

When she'd spent time in that hospital basement, they'd set up a TV with sitcoms for her to watch. Nothing current or stressful while she was healing. All feel-good shows. Most of them involved families. Wacky families, found families, birth families. Most a little unconventional and silly. But all with a solid core of love holding them together.

She wanted that and she'd found it here. After living with the Midnight Lake group for weeks, she wanted to keep it. Fiercely. The best way to do that would be to eliminate the threat. If that was even possible. These people made her believe it might be, and she hoped they were right.

If they weren't, she didn't know how she'd survive the heartbreak.

Flynn took her hand and tugged her over to another desk where there was a large monitor attached to a desktop computer. This was the one that was entirely off the grid. No internet connection. Everything uploaded by USB.

Completely secure.

A good place for their data.

Flynn tapped a few keys and pulled up the map.

Tessa gasped at the detail. "This is amazing. It's exactly like I pictured, exactly like I hoped. You're incredible."

She hugged him and he held her tight. "Most of the credit goes to Bella, but I'll definitely take the reward."

Tessa reached on her toes to kiss him, then dropped into the chair to study the map.

The street map showed Houston and the outlying areas. Colored overlays showed areas where various groups operated.

Yellow was the assigned color for Pavic and it fit. The family was sick and when the yellow overlaid the map, it took on a sickly tone.

She turned to Flynn. "Do you mind if I make some additions?"

He laughed and sat beside her. "We did it for you. Change, add, and delete at will."

"Thank you."

Flynn returned to where she'd been working, grabbed her headphones and notebook, then brought them to her.

He dropped a kiss on her head. "Work your magic, Tessa."

F lynn could feel Tessa's desperation to solve the problem from across the room. For two days, she'd been relentless in reading data and collating it into patterns only she could see.

She used numbers, diagrams, maps, and what she called web-spheres to pull it all together.

Flynn was no dummy, but it made his head spin. Her brain worked differently from anyone he'd met. Even Tansy, who invented things like spy gear and shuttle parts along with cleaning robots and dinosaur toys.

Over the past few days, Flynn had become familiar with Tansy, Bella, Mitch, and Aisling. He'd already known Sam and Graham, but getting to know the others had been good.

They made an excellent team. He wanted this case solved and Tessa safe so they could be part of the team permanently.

Joe, Nico, and Josie would arrive any time. He hoped the sketch artist could help them get some potential likenesses for Martin and Karlo.

Neither man had ever had a driver's license, so there were no photos to find online. One way to know they'd been born into a criminal family. Official photos were often missing or unidentifiable.

Fake beards, earrings, temporary tattoos, cheek implants, fake scar tissue, colored contacts. Any way to shield the face and interfere with facial recognition software. He knew a few people in jail who'd used movie-type enhancements to change their forehead or jawlines for pictures.

If Josie could get a clear picture from Tessa's descriptions, he hoped they would get a hit. Unless they'd gone the plastic surgery route. With the arrogance that emanated from the family, he doubted it. He hoped to prove one or both were alive.

Flynn's phone buzzed with a text from Nico. *Here.*

When he stood from his chair, Tessa glanced up. He motioned to the door and she pulled off her headphones. He walked over and held out his hand. "They're here."

She rolled her lips together and then nodded. Taking his hand, she stood. She didn't resist when he pulled her into a brief hug. "This is a good step. Come and meet everyone."

"Hey, Rodeo Man, stop mauling the girl and come on down."

Tessa's cheeks pinked, but she laughed with him as they headed down to the conference room.

Sam, Tansy, and Graham were with the new arrivals. Flynn hugged Josie first and then exchanged what he thought of as man-hugs with Joe and Nico.

He introduced Tessa. Her eyes widened when the three of them pulled her into hugs. Josie grinned at her. "So, you're the one who's got everyone in a tizzy. Nice to meet you. Who's going to tell us what the cloak and dagger is all about?"

Nico rolled his eyes. "Way to put her on the spot. How about a cup of coffee first? I always forget how cold it is up here."

Tessa looked at Josie. "It's a fair question, and I'm definitely the one in the center ring of this particular circus. It's a long story and there's no pressure. If it's too much to ask, that's okay. No hard feelings if someone isn't comfortable helping. It's a lot and I don't want anyone in danger because of me."

Her voice started strong, but wobbled a bit by the time she got to the end of her speech. Her eyes dropped to the ground and she turned to the stove. "I'll heat the kettle, too, if anyone wants tea."

While her back was turned, Josie turned to him and mouthed *Sorry*. The two men shot him a concerned glance as well.

Graham pulled out some cookies he'd baked along with some fruit and the next few minutes passed with catching up. When they were all seated around the table, Flynn took Tessa's hand in his. Her icy fingers trembled.

When there was a pause in the conversation, Tessa spoke. "Okay. This is hard for me, so I'm just going to blurt it out. I'm in Wit Sec. Have been since high school when my house exploded with me inside. I've since found out my grandfather, Grigor Pavic, is in charge of a criminal organization that may include my father and my uncles."

She squeezed his hand. "On the day of the explosion, my uncle falsely accused me of betraying the family, producing a journal I'd never seen as proof. I was beaten and tossed in a room for interrogation and possible rape when the house exploded. It was reported that I had died along with my father and uncle. I don't know if their deaths were faked as well."

She took a deep breath but didn't look up. "I spent several months in a coma and several years in a secure hospital recovering. I met Tansy through an FBI consult and I moved here a few months ago."

She looked at him with a soft smile. "Flynn and I were good friends in high school. It was a bit of shock when we saw each other a few days ago. I believe Pavic would know Flynn has an open file on the family and I believe he would keep track of him." Her voice wobbled again and she stopped.

Flynn took over. "We want to find a way to keep Tessa safe and here. The only way to do that is to eliminate the threat. Put Pavic in jail and take apart his organization."

Everyone nodded.

Joe leaned in. "This is the case you've been working on since joining the FBI? The one you've wanted to clear before joining Midnight Security full-time?"

"It is."

Joe grinned. "We're in. What's the plan?"

Tessa's mouth dropped open as she stared at Joe, then Nico, then Josie. They all smiled.

When Tessa didn't say anything, Flynn squeezed her hand again and spoke. "There are no reliable pictures of Martin Blanco or Karlo Pavic online. We'd like Josie to work with Tessa to see if they can come up with a likeness from when Tessa was in high school. Then we'll input that into facial rec software and see what we find."

"Are you sure?" Tessa's question was soft but everyone at the table nodded.

"We're sure." Josie grinned. "Taking down the shitheads is fun."

Nico rolled his eyes. "So eloquent. We've got the skills and the team. Show us what you've got and we'll figure out how to divide up tasks from there."

Tessa's eyes shone with tears but he watched her battle them back. "Thank you. If it gets too dangerous, I'll go and then you'll be safe."

Josie tilted her head. "Not used to people having your back, are you? Why don't you catch up everyone with the details and then you and I can get to the fun stuff?"

Flynn grinned and dropped a kiss on Tessa's head. "Told you they'd be in. Let's do this."

CHAPTER 15

Second Set Of Eyes

Tessa couldn't believe the activity around her. Aisling, Bella, and Mitch had joined the group and were helping as well.

Tansy had her magic bubble wrapped around the cabin to add an extra layer of security. People were scattered around the cabin working in small groups on research, collating data, improving the map, and other things she wasn't quite sure about.

She and Josie moved to a corner and Josie pulled out a sketchpad along with a large tablet that she powered up.

"I'm going to work on paper at first and then on the computer to refine it. Would it be easier to start with your uncle or your father?"

She didn't want to talk about her father yet. "I feel like there's more of a chance that my uncle's still alive, so let's start there."

Josie grinned. "Which neatly avoids the question. No worries. I don't pry. Okay, tell me what you remember most about good old Uncle Karlo."

"Besides the fact that he set me up to get beaten, raped, and killed?"

Josie's face softened and she dropped her pencil to pick up Tessa's hand. "I'm so sorry you went through that. He sounds like a total prick."

"He was. Or is." Tessa shook her head and blew out a breath. "Okay.

I'll get my head in the right space. I'm just overwhelmed by the generosity of people here."

Josie smiled as she looked around the room. "I hear ya. These are some excellent people you've hooked up with."

They shared a smile and then Josie picked up the pencil again. "Okay, let's start with you just describing him for me. Basic body type, height, clothing. That kind of thing. I'm going to hide my work from you. It tends to influence what people see in their memory. Close your eyes if you're a visual person."

Tessa frowned. "I'm more a numbers person than an art person. I don't know if I'm going to be able to do this at all."

Josie laughed. "No problem. That part's my job. I'll just turn up the magic and we'll see what we come up with. My first sketch will only be to get my brain working."

Josie's optimism was contagious and Tessa nodded. "Karlo was tall. Thin build. Strutted more than walked. Full head of hair. He was always vain about his hair."

"Slicked back?"

"No. More soft waves. Parted on the left. Wait, my left. His right."

"Any grey in his hair?"

Good question. Tessa tried closing her eyes again. "A little. Not much. Mostly dark brown, almost black."

"So dark eyes, too?"

"Yes." She'd never got closer to her uncle than had been necessary, so she couldn't remember the exact color.

Josie nodded and continued to sketch on her notepad. "Tell me about his personality, his clothes."

"Always dark suits when I saw him. Never in casual clothes. My father was the same. Appearances were always important." Which was why she preferred jeans and t-shirts these days.

"Any facial hair?"

"Not that I ever saw. Always clean shaven. Sharp jaw and nose."

"I bet his eyebrows were furrowed most of the time."

"Yes. How did you know?"

Josie raised an eyebrow and smirked. "I'm good. Plus you're painting the picture of a nasty, arrogant man. It was a pretty safe bet."

That surprised a laugh out of Tessa. "Sounds like you've got him, beady eyes and all."

Josie continued to ask questions, overall ones and not specifics as Tessa had imagined. Her lack of observational ability didn't appear to bother the artist at all.

Eventually, she whipped the sketchbook around without warning. Tessa heard herself gasp even as she backed away from the image.

It was a full body sketch and it made Tessa feel the tightness in her chest she'd always felt when she'd been in close contact with him.

The man loomed at her, disdain in every line of his body. Her breathing went shallow and her heart raced.

All from a sketch.

Flynn appeared at her side and grabbed her hand. "You okay?"

She blinked and yanked her eyes away from the sketch and to him. "Yes. I'm fine. Sorry."

Tessa looked over at Josie's smile. "You're right. You're good. Very, very good."

Flynn didn't even look at the sketch. Instead he studied her and stroked her hand.

Josie placed the pad on the table with the sketch facing down and patted her hand. "I'm going to get this into my computer program and we'll work to refine the details, especially the face. Why don't you take a break? It's an emotional hit from where you're sitting. Give me a half hour or so."

Flynn pulled her to her feet. "Let's take a walk."

She looked around the cabin where everyone was working. All to help her. "I should see where I can help."

He tugged her toward the door and she didn't resist. "A short walk outside isn't going to hurt. It'll help clear your head for Josie."

They slipped on boots and grabbed jackets, then stepped out into the cold. Snow was falling lightly and clouds covered the sky.

She drew in a deep breath of the chilly air and let the crispness fill her lungs. After the intensity of the last few hours, the simplicity of the icy air soothed her nerves.

Flynn took her hand and they walked toward the lake. Jetson barked behind them and loped across the snow to join them.

Ginger would be inside the main lodge, probably watching the snow from what had become her favorite spot beside the pellet stove in the main room.

The cat was wary of Spike and Willow, but was probably looking for her German Shepherd buddy who preferred being outside in the winter.

The cat had settled in as well as Tessa had. And Flynn. He fit right in with the group.

When she'd been tossed into a new life the first time, it had been emotionally painful. If it happened again it would be worse. So much worse.

Flynn stopped and wrapped his arms around her, linking them behind her back. "You're thinking too hard. Let's see if we can find a way to relax you."

Then his mouth was on hers. Hungry and hot. She gave into the kiss and let her nerves and fears be pushed away by the desire that hovered close to the surface whenever this man was near.

Flynn didn't move his hands, simply drove her to total distraction with his mouth, teasing her higher and higher while the snow fell around them.

Her body warmed, the tension melted away, and her heart filled. This man was everything she wanted.

I love you.

The words wanted to emerge, wanted to battle their way out of her heart and into the universe. But how could she say them when the future was so uncertain?

There was still a possibility that she would have to disappear and start over again. Telling Flynn would only hurt him in the long run.

So, she'd keep the words inside and fight like hell to get a normal life.

Flynn worked on the map with Bella and Mitch while Tessa finished with Josie. The artist was amazing. Josie kept the atmosphere light even as she pulled details of the two men from Tessa's past who may have planned her death.

Watching them across the room had pride for Tessa surging through him. She didn't balk from the ugly task.

Tansy had brought the cat back with her when she'd gone to the lodge for something and it sat in Tessa's lap as if it always had.

They'd been back to work for a few hours when Josie pushed back her chair and whooped. She did a little spin with her arms in the air and her head tossed back.

From the table beside him, Nico growled. "It's not a damn football game."

But when Flynn got up to cross the room, Nico followed him.

Tessa beamed up at them. "Josie is a genius."

Josie spun in her chair and laughed. "Only because you're so easy to work with. You noticed so much more than you thought you did. Your emotional memory is excellent."

Flynn leaned down and kissed Tessa's hair. "You finished?"

She smiled and nodded. Her eyes were weary but content. The stress from earlier had lessened. Definitely good news.

Josie clicked a few buttons on the laptop and her sketches of Tessa's father, uncle, and the thugs who'd been at the house that day filled the screen. They were labelled, but Flynn didn't need it to see the similarities between Tessa and her father. They had the same nose and forehead. The eyes were similar in shape and color, but Tessa's held all the emotions. Martin's were cold and blank. Even in the sketch. Flynn couldn't imagine growing up with those eyes for a role model.

Once again, he was impressed that Tessa had become such an amazing human being. He rubbed her shoulders softly, trying to impart how proud he was of her.

Nico frowned at the screen. "I assumed when you said your father and uncle that they were brothers. These men don't share many physical similarities."

While Josie seemed to bristle, Tessa looked up at Nico. "Karlo Pavic is my mother's brother. She died when I was too young to remember her."

Nico nodded and patted her shoulder. He turned to Josie. "Have you loaded them up yet?"

She rolled her eyes. "Impatient much? We just finished. I assume you're going to put them through on your credentials. I don't have the authorization to begin a search."

Nico frowned but nodded. "Send the results to my FBI email. I'll have to call in and get authorization."

Josie turned back to her computer and the rest of them moved away.

Flynn motioned for Tessa to follow him to where they'd been working on the map. They'd made great progress and input a ton of data. To Flynn, the map was a jumble of words and numbers. He hoped it would help Tessa figure out their next steps.

Her delighted gasp when she saw it had everyone around smiling.

Mitch grinned. "To me, it's like a massive doodle, but we've input pretty much every piece of data connected to the Pavic organization and color coded it."

Tessa grinned. "This is incredible. Can we put it up on the big screen?"

Soon, most of the group was staring at the map. Flynn wondered how many others found it more confusing than helpful. The way Tansy and Bella gravitated toward it, he assumed they were as delighted as Tessa.

When he heard the door close, he turned to find Nico striding back in. He must have made his phone call outside. He walked straight to Flynn. "Got it. Let's see where we can spot these bastards."

They couldn't access the classified search engines remotely, but they hoped the ones they could access would give them enough. If Martin and Karlo were alive, they had to believe the authorities thought them dead. After more than a decade, he'd bet they weren't as careful.

Graham let out a shrill whistle and waited until everyone looked at him. "I've got Marcus and Troy coming up the trail with enough food for everyone from the No Fail Diner. They'll be here in about twenty minutes. I vote we include them in our little group. We know they're reliable and discreet. If we don't want to include them, we'll need to head to the lodge in ten and make like we're having a welcome party for Rodeo Man."

Graham winked at Tessa. "No pressure, cutie. You've got eight minutes to decide."

Everyone chuckled and made an effort not to look at Tessa. Her eyes flew to Flynn's and she met him halfway across the room.

From previous conversations with his friends, he knew Marcus Ramirez was the local deputy and Troy Phail ran Phail General. Both men had military backgrounds and had proven themselves in earlier situations where the Midnight Security gang required backup.

"What do you think?" Tessa asked before he could ask her the same.

Flynn shrugged. "I think the more good people we have on our side, the better. And the sooner we'll be able to solve this. More importantly, what do you think? You know these guys. I've heard about them, but haven't met them yet."

Tessa nodded. "I don't know them as well as the others do, but they've proven themselves more than once." Her gaze moved around the room. "I've put so many people in danger just by being here."

"Hey." He waited until she looked back at him. "We've gone over this. Not your fault. Everyone here understands that. Everyone here wants to help and make the world better and safer. Taking down the Pavic family is the right thing to do."

He waited and watched as she stared into his eyes. She walked into his arms and nodded. "I wish I wasn't at the center of this whole mess, but I am, and it's time to be brave. Okay. Let's bring them in on it, too."

She squeezed him then stepped back and turned to Graham. "Okay."

Graham strode over and put his hands on her biceps, then lifted her to her toes. He kissed her on the lips with a large smacking noise and then released her. "In case you missed it, our group is getting bigger. Pavic is that much closer to going down."

Laughing, Tessa returned to Flynn's arms.

Graham's partner Aisling rolled her eyes and laughed as Graham moved back to where they were working. He kissed her hair and then winked back at Tessa.

Flynn found himself laughing too. The group might be a little wacky, but they were exactly the right people.

CHAPTER 16
Saddle Up

Tessa stared at the data, studied the map, then tapped her finger on the same spot. "I think I have something."

Her voice hadn't been loud, but suddenly the room was completely quiet. She'd trained herself not to be noticed. To be invisible and unremarkable. Having everyone listening to her wasn't comfortable, but it was part of being normal.

She sat on a tall stool in front of the large screen that showcased the map they'd been building. Using Josie's sketches, there had been no sightings of her father, but several potential sightings of Karlo in the Houston area.

She'd added those to her web-spheres while someone else had added them to the map. For the past twenty minutes, she'd been doubting her data and findings, but from every angle she looked, she came to the same conclusion.

Flynn appeared at her side. "What do you have?"

She tapped the screen again. "This building right here."

The air in the room stirred as everyone moved closer. It was almost midnight and they should be packing it in, but no one had wanted to break.

"That's in the Theater district?"

"It is. There's a ghost floor that isn't registered to anyone."

"Ghost floor?" Josie's voice was puzzled.

Tessa nodded. "It's a floor that's hidden behind the upper half of a two-story space." She enlarged the floor plan. "This ballroom is two stories in height, but it doesn't extend across the entire floor. There's a space in the back that has offices and those offices have regular ceiling heights. There's a floor above them, but it doesn't show up on the plan and it isn't leased to anyone."

Sam leaned back against her desk while he studied the map. "What brought you to this building?"

"The orange dots show the potential sightings of Karlo. Almost all of them are within a block of this address. And the corporation that owns this building is a shell company. One of the shell companies in the chain of money leading to that bank account attached to no identification. Probably Karlo. I believe it's a Pavic building and company."

Troy moved closer. "Do you think it's their headquarters? I assumed that would be in the mansion they own." He tapped the map with the location highlighted.

Tessa nodded. "I agree. I think this is one of their illegal gambling sites. They might have several, but this one isn't in any specific gang territory. The neighborhood is known for its nightlife and no one would notice people coming or going at all hours of the night."

The more she spoke, the more confident she felt. She went through the data and showed the financials. When she finally looked, most of the others nodded or smiled back at her.

Sam grinned. "Okay. Now we have a location and we're going to figure out how to use that place. We need a plan, but I think we need to sleep first. Troy and Marcus, why don't you find yourselves rooms for the night and we can pick it up in the morning."

Within twenty minutes, the data was secured and everything shut down. As everyone moved toward the door, Tessa stretched her legs. Sitting for so many hours was taking its toll on her legs and hips.

She used her hands to push off the desk and stood. Flynn arrived beside her again. "How can I help?"

"I'm good. Just a bit stiff."

He checked over his shoulder and then grinned. "Trust me?"

"Of course."

He swung her up into his arms. "We're the last ones in the cabin. Let me help you to the front door."

Flynn trotted down the stairs and when he reached the door, he slid her down his body. With a growl and a quick kiss, he helped her into her winter gear and put on his own. Then he grabbed the cat and tucked it into his jacket. It wasn't far to the lodge, but the wind took only seconds to leach the heat from a body.

Outside, Flynn locked the deadbolt and set the alarm. The wind had picked up since the last time they'd been outside and the snow whirled around them.

She shook her head at the sight. "Must be wonderful to be a kid in a place with snow. It's magical stuff."

"Until it tosses your car into a ditch or downs your power lines."

"I'm sure Tansy has a plan for the second one."

He laughed. "I'm sure she does. Do you have any of that girly stuff you put in a tub?"

"What?"

"You know. The bubble stuff. It's been a long day of sitting and I wondered if soaking in the bath would make your legs feel better."

This man. "You're so sweet."

He recoiled as if she'd cursed him. His growl was low. "I'm not sweet. Sweet is a piece of chocolate or one of those sappy movies."

Tessa laughed as they walked into the lodge. Ginger jumped down as soon as Flynn unzipped his jacket. She stalked off, probably in search of her buddy, Jetson.

Flynn helped Tessa off with her boots, and she wrapped her arms around him when he stood. "See. Sweet."

With another growl. He bent low and lifted her over his shoulder, then turned and jogged up the stairs to her room. She was still laughing when he closed the door. He stomped into her bathroom with her still hanging over his shoulder.

Flynn slid her slowly down his chest and every single cell in her body yearned for his touch.

Before her feet hit the ground, she looped her arms around his neck and kissed him. She felt his body hardened and he put his hands on her butt and pulled her in more tightly.

She gasped into the kiss at the friction and the sparks that lit at every touch. She should be exhausted, should only want to crawl into bed and sleep. But she wanted a whole lot more than that.

Flynn boosted her legs around his waist and dropped to sit on the edge of the tub. Without breaking the kiss, he plugged the drain and started the water running.

"Where's your girly stuff?"

She smiled into the kiss. "Mostly wrapped around you."

He laughed and hugged her tightly, then set her on her feet. "Grab your stuff and let's get you in to soak away the stiffness."

So sweet.

She reached under the sink to grab a bath bomb and Flynn's hands landed on her butt again, squeezing.

She turned and tossed the bomb into the bath and then moved to stand between his legs. While she kissed him, her hands undid the buttons of his shirt. His started on hers. His magic touch had her shivering, but not from cold. Need coursed through her.

Flynn had her naked in the time it took for her to remove his shirt and get his belt buckle undone. A rodeo buckle. "What's this?"

He barked out a laugh and she poked him in the belly. "Not that. The belt buckle. Is it special?"

Flynn sighed dramatically and tapped the buckle. "From the last rodeo I did."

"How old were you?"

He frowned. "Nineteen maybe. I quit during college when my course-load got serious. By then, rodeo was just for fun, but my aim was the FBI."

Because of her. She wrapped her arms around him and leaned her head on his chest. "I'm sorry your life plans got derailed because of me."

He held her biceps and leaned back from her so he could see her face. "For the last time, none of this is your fault. Stop feeling guilty. Stop apologizing. Shit happens. We deal with it and move on. If you can't move on, you're never really going to move past it all, Tessa. Let it go."

His intensity had her throat closing up. For a long moment, she simply looked into his eyes. She saw the passion for his job, his determination to make the world better.

She also saw his concern and his caring for her.

Love? Maybe not. But it was more than she'd ever hoped to see.

And if she wanted to nudge that caring into love, she did need to move on. Could she?

For this man? Absolutely.

Flynn wanted to head down to the FBI office in Houston and get to work. They'd have better access to programs and the support of the team. He wanted tactical input and a coordinated plan set up with local PD.

He also wanted to stay at Midnight Lake and keep Tessa safe in his arms forever. If he accomplished the first, he hoped he could have the second.

He'd left Tessa up in her room doing the stretches she required to move freely and had come down for coffee. Except they only had tea in the lodge.

Tansy had a stash of organic types stacked in jars on a kitchen shelf. He set the kettle on the pellet stove and decided that the ginger-lemon smelled like it had enough of a kick for him. He'd grab a coffee when they headed over to the Midnight Security cabin.

Nico walked into the kitchen and pulled down another mug. "Come to any conclusions?"

Straight to it. Flynn leaned back against the counter. "Now that we have a potential target and a visual, I think we'd be better off moving down to the Houston office and working out of there. Pull in more resources. Double-check our data with their systems."

Nico nodded and they moved to sit by the stove while waiting for the water to heat. "I agree. It shouldn't be any problem for me and Joe to join the team. And Sam. Even though he's turned in his badge, he's done some contract work for the field office up here."

Flynn nodded. Sam's reputation alone should allow him access to the building and the team. "I want to talk to Tessa first, and then I'll put in a call to my director, see if we can set it up."

Nico crossed his long legs at the ankles. It was odd to see his buddy in anything other than a suit, but he didn't appear uncomfortable in the moccasins and jeans. "We can't leave everyone here unprotected."

That thought worried Flynn as well. How could he be sure Tessa was safe if she wasn't with him? But he couldn't risk taking her to Houston. Someone had tried to kill her there once.

Graham and Mitch would be here. Bella was trained with a gun and knew how to use it. He didn't know if Tessa knew how to shoot. Or Aisling or Tansy.

Graham had a shooting range at the Midnight Runway property, but if they wanted surprise on their side, they'd need to move quickly and there wouldn't be sufficient time to train everyone.

The security measures the team had installed on the property were great for alerting them to problems, but they wouldn't solve them.

"Sounds like you're planning a trip."

Flynn turned to find Tessa watching them.

She frowned at the two of them. "Tell me you weren't planning to go all caveman."

"Caveman?"

"The men ride off into the sunset while the women sit home and wring their helpless little hands."

Nico laughed and stood from his chair. He gestured for Tessa to take his spot as he headed out of the room. "My cue to leave."

Tessa moved closer but didn't sit. "Tell me what you're planning."

He took her hand. "Nothing nefarious. If you'd been earlier, you would have heard me tell Nico I needed to talk to you first."

She sat in Nico's seat and didn't let go of his hand. "Tell me."

He nodded. "I think we've reached the action stage. Mostly thanks to you, we've gathered a lot of intel. The next stage is to check out the intel and see if we're right in our assumptions."

"Check it out. As in, go to Houston and see."

He nodded again. "Yes. I'd like to bring the information we've collected to my director, Janis Jenkins. Joe, Nico, and Sam would likely come with me. We'd assemble a team, work with other divisions within the FBI and local PD. Then we'd figure out the best way to take down the Pavic family."

"If it was that easy, why hasn't it been done before?"

Flynn shifted and took both her hands. "A couple of reasons. Mostly, there are bigger problems. Plus, we've never had the data to give us an advantage. You've given us that. That's why I'm hoping the director will approve an operation."

She frowned. "They might not?"

He shrugged. "There's always a battle for where to best spend the resources. Everyone wants to use the people and time in the most effective way. With the information we've collected and the theories we have, I hope that's enough."

"And if it's not?"

"Let's not go down that pathway until we don't have any other option. I think this will work. Jenkins is smart and tough. She hates the red tape as much as anyone. She also knows how to use a weapon when it's put in her hand. We're going to be handing her that weapon with all the data. I believe she'll be willing to use it."

"Okay. When do we leave?"

Fear grabbed onto Flynn's heart. "*We* don't. At least not you. You'll stay here. Jenkins isn't going to let civilians in on the op."

She shook her head. "No. This is my problem. I need to be part of the solution. If anyone goes to Houston, I'm going, too."

"It's too dangerous."

"I'm not suggesting I pick up a gun and walk into the casino announcing I'm looking for my grandfather. But I know the data and I can help."

"You'll be safer here. And we have these new inventions called cell phones. You can be in the loop and safe."

She rolled her eyes. "I wasn't asking your permission."

Then she rose and walked stiffly toward the back hallway. Jetson rose from his spot by the fire and sent Flynn a glare. Then the dog followed her down the hall.

CHAPTER 17

Bucked Off

Tessa wished her body could run. It seemed like a good way to purge the fear and mad out of her system. She knew Flynn wasn't being an ass, but she was still pissed. He didn't want her in Houston because he didn't think she would be an asset. He figured she was a liability and they'd be better with her out of the way.

Okay, he hadn't said any of that, but that's how she felt. For years, she'd wanted to know answers, but had been too afraid to dig. Now she was digging. Finding answers. Acting like part of a team. It was new for her and she liked it. A lot.

She didn't want to shrink back into her small life. She liked this bigger life, filled with people she cared about. The only way to keep this new life was to fight for it. She didn't need to fight Flynn. She needed to fight her own insecurities and the limitations she'd imposed on herself.

Stay hidden. Don't be noticed. Don't call attention to yourself. Don't react.

Don't. Don't. Don't.

This was her chance to Do. And she wasn't going to miss it.

Tessa laced up her boots and tossed on a jacket. At the last second, she remembered a hat and gloves. Jetson stood when she opened the back door and trotted outside with her.

Creeping down the snow-covered stairs reminded her of those limitations, but she kept going into the chilly air. She walked toward the lake where only a few days ago she'd been measuring habitats for turtles slumbering in the lake. A day when she hadn't yet met Flynn for the second time.

She wasn't even sure how many days ago that had been. A week? Two? Regardless of the time, she'd gone through a transformation and she didn't want to go back. Couldn't go back. It was time to start actually living a life instead of a half-life. Act instead of react.

Jetson nudged her hand and she reached down to pet him. His tail wagged like it was on a motor. "Want to play?"

The dog loved to fetch, but the snow covered up any sticks she could throw for him. "How about a snowball? You want to chase that?"

It turned out Jetson loved chasing snowballs. She lobbed them in the air and he tried to catch them. When the snow covered his face, he danced with joy.

By the time her arm ached, she was smiling too.

"How about snow angels, Jetson? I need a break."

Knowing getting up from the snow wouldn't be fun, but wanting to do it anyway, Tessa slowly lowered herself to the ground and laid back. Jetson enjoyed the new game and bounced all around her, licking her face.

When she started moving her arms and legs in the traditional snow angel dance, Jetson bounced higher, trying to get between her arms and legs. Laughter bubbled out of her and it felt too good to try to stop.

"One of my favorite sounds in the universe." Flynn's soft voice warmed her as well.

Jetson ran off to greet him and soon the two of them were beside her. She kept her arms and legs moving in the pattern when Flynn appeared to grin down at her. "Snow angels?"

She smiled back. "I've never made one before. Seemed like the thing to do."

He grinned and sat down in the snow beside her. Then he followed her lead and made his own snow angel.

She reached for his hand and for a few moments, they simply moved their limbs in sync and enjoyed the peace of the morning and the silly dog running around them and having a great time.

Flynn broke the silence. "I'm sorry I upset you."

Tessa huffed out a breath. "I know. And I know you weren't trying to. I get it. I know I'm a liability in so many ways."

In a flurry, Flynn was sitting up and looking down into her face. "You're in no way a liability. You're incredibly smart, endlessly kind and thoughtful. Gorgeous too, but that's not the point."

But it made her smile.

His gloved hand brushed snow off her nose and skimmed over her lips. "I want desperately to keep you safe, Tessa. Nothing is more important to me. Nothing. I don't know how to do my job and protect you at the same time."

"I've been protecting myself for a long time." When he frowned, she reached up and took his hand. "It's amazing to have you worried. To have you thinking about me. I'm used to being alone. It's taking me some time to adjust."

His grin reappeared. "I'll try to curb my caveman tendencies, but you're important, Tessa. I don't want you in any danger."

Jetson barked, annoyed that they'd stopped the snow angel game.

They both ignored the dog as Flynn reached down to kiss her lightly. He sat back and looked at her seriously. "We'll figure it out together, Tessa. With the help of our team. We'll put a plan in place that everyone can live with."

She nodded while Jetson continued to bark. "Could you call your boss from inside the Midnight Security cabin with Tansy's protection stuff in place? Or does it work that way? I haven't asked. That way, we could get her input before making any final decisions. If we know she can't help, we won't waste time getting to Houston."

Flynn nodded then Jetson moved between them and barked again. She was about to shove him playfully away when the dog's stiff body language registered. "What's wrong, boy? Is something wrong?"

Flynn jumped up instantly and looked around while Tessa started to move. The cold had leached into her body and her movements were slow and awkward.

Jetson continued to bark, but she couldn't see anything he might be barking at. Then the mechanical hum registered. "Do you hear that? Jetson, quiet."

Flynn froze as well and they both looked around for the source of the hum.

She'd managed to sit, but she couldn't identify anything moving around them. "What is it?"

Jetson barked again and then howled up to the sky.

And she saw it. A drone hovered over them. With the way the dog was reacting, not one of Tansy's.

Flynn swore as his phone rang. When he thumbed it open, Sam's voice rang out. "Drone. Get inside. Don't look up. Move but be casual."

Tessa realized if someone had been looking for confirmation she was at Midnight Lake, the snow angels had given them a perfect way to capture her face.

She started to push to her feet, but Flynn scooped her up and kissed her even while he moved to the lodge, the dog at their feet.

Horror and terror kept her from protesting Flynn's actions. Her carelessness had cost them all. Not only had she allowed herself to be identified, but she'd painted a giant target on Midnight Lake.

F lynn set a shaking Tessa on her feet as soon as they were inside. He didn't bother taking off his boots before he hollered. "Team meeting. Now."

Then he moved to the main room and to the side of the window. He couldn't see the drone from where he stood, but it was there. And it had more than enough opportunity to capture Tessa's image.

People moved in from the workout room and feet thumped down the stairs. Everyone except Sam and Tansy appeared.

He grabbed his phone from the pocket he'd stuffed it into. Sam was still on the line. He tapped the screen. "You're on speaker phone. I've got everyone here. Are you at the fort?"

He'd learned that Tansy had a cabin another mile or so further into the property. It was where she worked on her projects, especially the ones that required additional security or quiet.

Sam's voice came from the phone while the others gathered around. "Yes. A few hours ago, Tansy had an idea about additional security. She's programmed the drones to take random flights throughout the day and night, to report unusual activity in the air and on the ground."

Tansy spoke next. "We came out here to work on it. I had to program them to ignore the natural movements of birds and animals. It's a complicated bit of programming and I didn't finish soon enough. I'm sorry."

Flynn shook his head at that. "Nothing to be sorry about. I'll just catch everyone up. Tessa and I were playing outside with Jetson. She was doing snow angels when the drone flew over. Jetson noticed it before we realized why he was barking. It had ample time to take images of our faces."

There was a beat of silence while everyone absorbed the implications of that.

Sam spoke again. "We're packing up here. The drone hovered for a few minutes and then headed south, but not toward Phail, somewhere west of that. We'll be there soon, but that's the basics."

The phone cut off and Flynn imagined they were running. It wouldn't take them long and they knew how to hide in the bush.

Aisling spoke up. "Graham and I will go grab the laptops from Midnight Security. Might be easier to monitor the security system with them as well as our phones."

Joe held up his phone. "I'll call Shanice Williams." The lead agent in Bedford would be able to help if needed.

Marcus nodded. "I'll alert nearby deputies."

Flynn's heart swelled with pride for this team. He definitely wanted it to be his permanent home. "I'll call my boss in Houston and fill her in. See if she's got any new intel on Pavic or has heard about any movement."

The team spread out and Flynn headed to the workout space to get some quiet. He'd have to explain the entire mess to Jenkins and hope she wouldn't be pissed he'd been working on something without keeping her in the loop. Being on vacation wouldn't cut it as an excuse.

It took him over thirty minutes, but he talked her down from squashing him like a bug. She already had people checking out Pavic's empire and the ghost floor, and would update him with any new intel.

He realized he should have suggested Tessa call John Tynan, her US Marshal handler and clue him into the situation as well. Damn. She'd probably thought of it on her own.

He headed back to the main room to find the team working on different laptops. Tansy and Sam were back. The FBI men stood to the side, so he moved that way to catch them up on his call.

Joe nodded as he summed up what Jenkins was working on. "Shanice Williams is mobilizing a small unit to Phail. They'll come in like a group of friends vacationing." Williams was the lead agent over in New Hampshire, the closest FBI office.

Flynn looked at his friends. "We're all assuming an attack will come quickly?"

Nico nodded. "If it's Pavic or one of his men, and there's no reason to think it might be someone else, then we have to assume he'll react as soon as he has enough information."

It was good having a profiler at your back and they all listened as Nico continued. "I doubt it would be Grigor Pavic, but it might be Karlo or Martin acting as his peon. Because they're not in the system, they're both likely candidates. Grigor is the type to ensure that his people fix their own mistakes. And he would view Tessa being alive as a mistake. It could be another thug, but everything I've been reading leads me to believe it's Karlo using his new persona of Karl Kuzmetzov out there."

Nico's voice dropped. "I don't have any evidence pointing to Martin being alive, but we should remain alert to that possibility as well."

Flynn wondered how Tessa would feel either way. It seemed there were only a few possibilities. Either her father had set her up to be killed or he'd been killed in the blast. It was possible Martin was deep undercover, but Flynn suspected that Grigor's own son was the one who'd set up Tessa and caused the explosion along with her father's death.

No matter how this turned out, this was going to be difficult for her.

Flynn scanned the room to find her when Tansy called out. "Our drone has caught activity in the southwest quadrant. An SUV has pulled over beneath the trees near the fence."

Off the highway, away from Phail.

Sam moved to stand behind Tansy where he could see the screen. She pointed at something and he nodded. "Looks like a small team. Maybe three or four."

Joe called out. "How much time do we have, Tansy?"

She frowned at her screen, then looked up. "Probably less than fifteen minutes if you want to be in place before they arrive."

Her brother nodded. "We do. Grab whatever you need from your rooms and be back here in five minutes."

As everyone started to move, Flynn got a look at the group and his heart froze.

They were one person short.

"Where's Tessa?"

CHAPTER 18

First Strike

T essa stared at the wall and tried to breathe. The air kept clumping in her throat, choking her. She closed her eyes and focused. Slow. Easy.

"Tessa?" The door banged open and Flynn flew into her bedroom. His eyes were wide and full of fear.

When they made eye contact, his eyes closed and his entire body sagged. He didn't slow down, but ended up on the floor in front of her on his knees. He grabbed her hands and kissed them. "I thought you were gone. You scared the hell out of me."

She nodded and swallowed hard. "I should be gone. I should still go. If I leave, everyone here will be safe. But I can't force myself to do it. How selfish does that make me?"

"You're not in the least bit selfish. I'm so glad you didn't leave."

"I brought them here. I brought danger to you. To everyone here." She couldn't blink away the tears.

Flynn framed her face with his hands. "No. If anything, they followed me, not you."

She shook her head. "They only followed you because they wanted to find me."

"And you told me that from the beginning. You're not at fault here.

And neither am I. This lands firmly at the feet of Grigor Pavic and the jerks who work for him."

She wished that was true.

Flynn kissed her lightly. "We'll have time to debate the finer points later. For now, we need you and your brain. We're making a plan to capture them. With all the research you've done, you've got the best idea of how they work. Help us stop them."

She had to help. It was her fault. Slowly, she nodded and then pushed to her feet. After a long look, she moved to the closet and replaced her go-bag with her new credentials into the secret space. She clicked it closed, but it would be there if leaving became the best option. For now, it was time to be brave and face the others.

In the main room, everyone appeared to be busy. Some were checking out weapons and gear, others worked on laptops and tablets. Still others clustered around a large monitor.

As Tessa and Flynn walked in, most of them looked up and smiled or nodded. No angry glares. No furrowed brows. Nothing to indicate they were holding her accountable for this incursion. The chatter was energetic and confident. For many of them, this was their job and they knew what they were doing.

Flynn rubbed her back and whispered. "Told you."

When she glanced at him, he waggled his eyebrows and she managed a small smile.

Sam's voice became clear as they joined the group around the monitor. "These guys are likely used to city life and city tactics. How can we use the woods to our advantage?"

Tessa thought of the turtles and the different depths. "Three-dimensional thinking. They might not think of looking up unless they're dealing with buildings and windows."

Flynn grinned. "Did you just make a Star Trek reference?"

She nodded. "Wrath of Khan. Best of the bunch."

He planted a noisy kiss on her. "You really are perfect."

She rolled her eyes, but his words and the warm chuckles around the room had her relaxing.

Tansy pointed at the screen. "It's winter so you'll only have the conifers. This area where you've added the obstacle course should be along their path. You could use the course to your advantage as well."

Tessa had visited the course a few times. They'd created a training facility using many of the natural elements of the forest. Several fallen trees had been turned into balance beams at varying heights, leading in a dizzying array through the trees. Her own body wasn't up to traveling it, but she'd seen most of the others zip through the course like monkeys.

Those with law enforcement backgrounds geared up as they finalized plans for their trap.

Flynn turned to her. "Anything else you can think of, Tessa?"

She nodded. "A couple of things. If they were smart, they'd be waiting until dusk, when the light is tricky or even night. They might simply be scouting the area or they might be armed with something big and long distance."

Sam nodded. "Like a bomb or a fire?"

She agreed. "If either my father or uncle are out there, they won't be in front. They'll let their team face the danger, so be prepared for someone well behind the others."

They all nodded.

"And they'll be ruthless. They won't give up easily. Please be careful. I don't want any of you getting hurt because of me." She refused to think worse than hurt.

They all shrugged off her words as they finished donning protective equipment and loading weapons. They all wore white jackets to provide some camouflage against the snow.

It made her stomach hurt and her heart ache. She forced her feet to remain planted on the floor rather than running to Flynn and begging him to stay.

As if sensing her thoughts, Flynn lifted his head to her. He crossed to her in a few steps and leaned down to kiss her lightly. "Have faith. We'll see you soon."

Tansy leaned back from where she'd hugged Sam. "You've all got the earpieces I made? Keep them open. We'll monitor from here and relay any information."

And then they were moving. Aisling closed the door behind them and locked it. Spike and Willow circled her and she bent to rub them.

The tension in the room was thick, but Tessa appeared to be the only one edging toward panic.

"Tessa? I could use your help."

Tessa looked to where Tansy was working at the computer. Her friend patted the seat next to her and Tessa moved over. She sat and looked at the screen where dots were moving across the map.

"I'm testing new tracking devices. I've added them to the jackets Sam keeps for all the training missions. The dots are our guys. I'd like you to watch the movements of the other men on the laptop. You won't have the dots to help, but I'm hoping you can spot them through the trees. Or by the way the trees move. You're good at analysis. See if you can figure out their plan from the way they move."

Tessa didn't know if Tansy was making up the task to keep her from that total panic or if she really could use her help. Either way, it was what she needed.

Taking a moment to clear her mind and drop into analyst mode, Tessa turned her attention to the laptop.

She needed to find a way to help.

Flynn jogged through the bush with Joe, Nico, and Sam. They'd split into two teams of four, working with the people they knew best. Graham, Troy, Marcus, and Mitch were on the other team.

Unless there were more cars on their way, the good guys outnumbered the bad guys. Hopefully outsmarted them too.

The big question mark was weapons. What were these people planning? Were they hoping to destroy the lodge along with anyone in it? That seemed an extreme way to take out a single person, but it wouldn't surprise him. They'd already blown up one house in an attempt to kill Tessa.

Flynn's team arrived at the training area that included a natural obstacle course. He hadn't seen it yet, but the others had described it as they ran.

Fallen trees had been woven into a crisscross arrangement that led into and around the trees. There were also areas where they'd piled large rocks and branches to use in strength training. A couple of ladders had been set high between limbs to offer upper body work.

There was more, but those were the pieces they planned to use to lure and trap the intruders.

Flynn swung himself up with one ladder, then clambered into the branches of the nearest pine. Nico followed suit with another ladder. Joe and Sam used the crisscrossing fallen trees to climb quickly beyond where most would look.

Sam had tossed Flynn a net from the garage on the way out. They hoped the surprise of something falling on them would give them an advantage. The net was several old badminton and volleyball nets woven together to create a larger unit. It wouldn't hold anyone for long, but the confusion it would create could be invaluable.

Tansy spoke through the earbud. "I see three men moving toward the training ground. Graham, Sam's team is all in place. If you spread your team between them and the lodge, you should be able to surround the group."

They hadn't wanted to risk voices traveling in the bush, so none of them would speak unless necessary. He wanted to know the weapons situation, but didn't want to risk it.

A few moments later, Tessa spoke through the ear bud. "They're moving in an arrow formation with one in front. We can't identify faces or much else. They all appear to be armed with handguns and one has a large pack strapped on his back. Potentially a long gun in there. Thicker barrel. Not sure what it is."

Tansy chimed in. "They're continuing to head straight for your position. Probably five minutes out. Maybe less."

Snow started falling in large fluffy flakes. Pretty, until the wind kicked up and smashed them into his face. He slowly shifted his position to keep his vision free.

If the intruders were from Texas, they probably weren't used to dealing with snow. It would keep them distracted and probably stop them from looking up. All good news.

Unfortunately, he wasn't used to dealing with snow either. Neither were a few of the others. At least they were outfitted with Sam's stock of winter gear.

Tessa spoke again. "They'll be entering the clearing momentarily. Still in arrow formation. The man on your left is about a step ahead of the man on your right. All within a few feet of each other. They haven't given any indication they know you're there."

Perfect.

The bushes at the edge of the clearing rustled and a man stopped at the edge, keeping himself mostly in the trees. In moments, the other two approached and stood on either side of the central man. Each looked around the clearing slowly. None of them looked up. Score one for Tessa and Spock.

The trio moved into the clearing in a tight formation, keeping their weapons up and scanning. His team remained frozen in place, knowing that any movement attracted attention. Snow swirled and slammed into everyone. The men below each took their hands off their weapons to wipe their faces every few steps. None of his team moved.

Of course, the men didn't aim directly for where Nico and Flynn held the net, but moved into the middle of the clearing, leaving themselves wide open if Flynn's group was ready to shoot to kill.

Was it a weird strategy he didn't understand or stupidity?

Even newbies to the bush should realize staying under cover was smarter. Maybe they didn't expect anyone to know they were there.

Two edged closer to him and Nico while the other continued down the center. Flynn slowly turned his head just enough to see his partner while keeping an eye on those below. Nico smiled in acknowledgement as Tessa started a countdown in their heads.

"Five, four, three, two, one."

They dropped the net onto the two men and immediately swung themselves lower using the ladders.

The third man whirled at the cursing behind him and raised his gun.

Sam tackled him from behind and Flynn turned his attention to the two beneath the net.

A shot whistled past his ear at the same moment he heard Tessa yell his name.

He called out. "FBI. Lower your weapons." As he rolled to the side, he heard the others yelling out as well, identifying themselves and calling for surrender.

The guy who'd made the shot shoved at the net and twisted to get Flynn in his sights. It wasn't a face he recognized from Josie's sketches.

Flynn raised his weapon before the other man could steady his shot. "Drop it unless you want a bullet between the eyes."

The thought of the paperwork involved had Flynn hoping the guy listened. They wanted answers, not bodies.

Their other team rushed into the clearing with weapons up and ready. They watched the perimeter while Flynn's team gathered weapons and used zip ties to secure the men.

None of the men matched the sketches. Probably thugs for hire. Irritation ran through Flynn. He'd been so sure they'd find Karlo in the group. Where the hell was he and who was calling the shots?

Tansy spoke. "Sam? Are you okay? Is everyone okay?"

Sam reassured her they were all fine.

The takedown had lasted maybe forty-five seconds. It didn't match what Flynn had expected. He looked around the clearing and checked the woods, expecting more people to approach. "Anyone else coming from the road, Tessa?"

"No. Just these three."

Where the hell was Kuzmetzov? Flynn didn't recognize any of these men from their research. Thugs for hire? He could see Pavic bringing along his own crew, but he imagined Kuzmetzov wouldn't have access to the same kind of money. Would he hire local and send them off to capture Tessa?

Sam and Nico were going through jackets and pockets. Nico held up a phone, but then shook his head. "Burner and no calls so far. I'll run the number, see if we get lucky and they bought some in bulk. That would at least nail down a location. See if they're locals."

Tessa's voice came through again. "Did you check to see if any of them has an explosive device on them?"

Sam answered. "Nothing. Empty pockets. No suicide vests."

That one hadn't crossed Flynn's mind. They didn't get a lot of that in organized crime where religion wasn't a factor.

Marcus spoke up. "Let's get these men inside and we can figure out what the hell is going on. The sawmill's closer. Let's head that way."

They hoisted the silent and sullen men to their feet. They'd only gone a few yards when Tansy spoke again. "There's a security breach coming from the area behind the Midnight Security cabin."

The exact opposite side of the lodge from where they stood. Flynn's blood froze in his veins.

Tessa chimed in. "Looks like four men. Armed and headed for the lodge."

Adrenaline raced through him as he turned away from the men they'd captured. This whole thing had been a diversion, a way to pull them away from the lodge. From Tessa.

Troy called out. "I have these guys. Go."

Flynn didn't question it. He was already running.

CHAPTER 19

Second Helping

Tessa's heart slammed into her ribs as she watched the two laptop screens. One showed the men who wanted to kill her, the other showed the man she loved and their friends. The attackers were moving steadily from beyond the edge of the lake toward the lodge. They were going to arrive well before Flynn's group.

Aisling looked at the screen and then around the room. "We're completely vulnerable in this room. There aren't any curtains on the main floor. We need to head up. I'll check the doors and turn off the lights. Grab whatever we might need."

Bella spoke up. "I've got my gun upstairs, and I'll grab the others from the safe."

Feeling guilty and useless, Tessa looked around, trying to find a way to help. "I'll get the cat and the laptops." The dogs at least would come when called. Tessa scooped up Ginger from her favourite spot by the stove.

Tansy moved to the back room. "I've put some reactive programming into the CleanySaurs. I'll activate those and be right up."

Josie stood with her hands on her hips. "I don't think my sketchpad is going to be much use. How about I channel some Home Alone tricks?"

Tessa marvelled at the group's calm and determination. She couldn't be surrounded by better people. She sent Josie a shaky smile. "Maybe grab some spice jars from the kitchen."

Josie grinned. "And some knives and rolling pins. On it."

They gathered on the second floor to assess the situation. The hallways were wider than the opening to the stairs, so they could hide on either side without being seen. Tessa put Ginger in her room and closed the door.

The three dogs followed Tansy up the stairs. "CleanySaurs are on duty. Hopefully, they'll provide a distraction and give the team time to get here."

Bella nodded. "We've got them outnumbered. We just need to be smart and stay safe. Who can handle a gun?"

Tansy shook her head sharply and grabbed a laptop.

Aisling held out her hand. "I've been practicing with Graham out at the Runway. I'm not great, but I won't shoot anyone on our team."

Bella laughed. "Good to know. Josie? Tessa?"

Josie shook her head. "Not a chance."

Tessa reluctantly nodded. The Marshals had trained her in gun safety while she'd been recovering in that hospital basement. She didn't like guns, but knew they might be necessary today. She took a few moments to familiarize herself with the weapon and locked on the safety. "Maybe we should retreat to the third floor. They'll probably search each floor before they move up."

"Good plan."

Before they started to move, Tessa spoke again. "I've got a small secret room in my closet. Aisling knows how to operate it. Three of you should be able to fit, although it'll be tight."

The four immediately shook their heads. "We're in this together."

Her heart slammed against her ribs and her voice wobbled. "But it's all because of me. I've brought these men here. I don't want any of you to be hurt because of me. Please."

Josie moved in to hug her. "I know I'm new to the group, but screw that. This isn't your fault. It's the fault of the assholes out there. We've just got to stall them until our trained team shows up." Then she grinned. "You know, if Nico had promised me some action, I might not have been as reluctant to come."

There was a pause as the double-meaning of Josie's words hit them all. Josie's face flushed deeply while the rest of them grinned.

"I didn't mean it that way." But the twinkle in her eye made Tessa wonder if maybe she did.

Josie laughed and waved her spice jars. "Get your minds out of the gutter and your asses up the stairs."

They all moved, and no one heeded Tessa's pleas to hide.

At the top of the stairs, Bella pulled the doors almost closed. "That should make it seem darker up here, easier for us to see them than for them to see us. But if we need to get into a room, it'll be easier."

They moved to the edges of the hallway, in sight of the stairs, but hopefully out of view.

Aisling moved to hug Willow. "I'm going to put the dogs in one of the rooms."

Tansy nodded as she looked at her laptop. "Use mine. It's farthest away. Hurry. They're sneaking onto the deck."

Aisling locked away Willow and Spike, but Jetson refused to leave his spot at the top of the stairs.

Tansy spoke into her microphone and updated the outdoor team on the status. "They're a few minutes out. We'll have to hold them off."

Bella's voice was steady. "We've got this."

Tessa wished she had Bella's confidence. She wanted to run and hide, but she couldn't leave everyone else to clean up her mess. Her job was to protect her friends. Nothing else mattered.

A burst of gunfire, breaking glass, and banging doors filled the air. Tessa yelped, but managed to keep the scream inside.

Jetson appeared to be the only one who didn't react. He kept his eyes trained on the stairs.

Tansy's voice was a shaky whisper as she reported the breach to the team and added, "Stay safe."

Josie opened the spice jars and passed them around. From downstairs, a male voice yelled in surprise or fear and more gunfire erupted from the main floor.

Tansy whispered with a grin. "Score one for the CleanySaurs."

That brought another round of smiles and eased the tension down a notch, although it was thick enough for Tessa to taste..

Feet sounded on the stairs below them. The old wood made it impossible to move up or down without noise. This sounded like several men. At the second floor, the steps paused. Voices drifted up, but not loud enough for her to distinguish the words.

More creaks indicated at least one was on his way up. Tessa clamped her teeth together to stop from yelling out. She wasn't sure if she wanted to scream at the man to go away or at her friends to hide. Flashes of those horrific moments in her house before it exploded threatened to overwhelm her. Only the fear for her friends helped her stay in the real world and not disappear into the panic.

When the creaks neared the top, Jetson growled low in his throat from where he crouched, watching the stairs.

Gunfire erupted and Tessa cried out the dog's name. He didn't yelp in pain and she strained to hear past the ringing in her ears for other sounds. When a gun barrel appeared, she tossed the spices from her jar where she hoped his face would be.

The gun disappeared and she could hear coughing, swearing, and thumping. Hopefully he broke his leg as he tumbled back down the stairs. More cursing followed and then more shots.

Tessa's entire body shook as she hauled Jetson to her side, out of the range of bullets. Tossing the spice mix at the man had been hard enough. How difficult would it be to shoot someone? To kill?

Her stomach tightened and she hugged the dog hard as she picked up her gun again.

Another gun barrel appeared and her friends reacted. More spices flew from other jars. A rolling pin flew past her. From the swearing, she guessed both hit their target.

"Stupid bitch." The scream sent chills over her body and into her heart. She knew the voice. She knew the hate in it.

Uncle Karlo.

"This time you'll stay dead."

When the gun appeared in her viewpoint, she took aim and fired as Jetson launched himself into the air.

Flynn slipped in the back door with Sam, Joe, and Nico on his heels. Gunshots fired upstairs, so they flew that way.

On the second landing, a man lay on the ground wiping his face and coughing while searching for his gun that lay next to a rolling pin. Flynn kicked the gun backward and leapt over him knowing someone else would deal with him.

From up the stairs, another man screamed "This time you'll stay dead." It had to be Pavic or Kuzmetzov.

Two shots fired while he started up the stairs and Tessa screamed.

Flynn's heart stopped beating and everything turned numb. Jetson's barking had him moving in less than a second but he'd never forgive himself if that partial second cost Tessa her life.

A man stumbled down the stairs backwards as Jetson landed on his chest and then leaped away. Flynn grabbed the man before he fell. He wrapped his arm around the man's throat and pressed his gun to his temple. "Drop it."

The man tried to jerk out of the hold and his elbow rammed into Flynn's ribs, but Flynn didn't give ground. Not when Tessa's life was at stake.

He tightened his arm enough to let the asshole know he was deadly serious. "Drop it or die. Right here, right now." And then he tightened his arm again.

The gun clattered to the stairs and Flynn dragged him down to the landing before passing him to Nico and racing up the stairs with Sam.

"Tessa!" His voice broke as he ran. "It's us."

He kept his gun at his side, hoping he didn't have to use it, that no one dangerous had made it to the third floor.

As he crested the stairs, he found Tessa and the other women ready to face down any threats. "You're okay? Are you okay?"

Peripherally, he noticed everyone nodding, but he only had eyes for his Tessa. He swooped her into his arms and held her, reveling in the beating of her heart. "You're okay."

Tessa nodded into his chest and he turned to survey the group. A couple of guns, knives, spices, and another rolling pin. "Nice arsenal, ladies. You're amazing."

From where she was wrapped in Sam's arms, Tansy smiled. "We had a couple of CleanySaurs who helped out, too."

From below them, Nico's voice called out. "All clear. Prisoners in the main room. Backup on the way."

Flynn holstered his gun and grabbed Tessa's hand. He wasn't letting her out of his sight. Her hand shook and he realized she was holding a gun with her other hand. Eyes wide, she looked up at him. "I shot at him. I didn't kill him, did I?"

Flynn shook his head. "No. He was alive and cursing when Nico cuffed him. I didn't notice any wounds but I was in a hurry to get here. I assume that was your uncle or your grandfather." He'd been in such a hurry, he hadn't even noticed the man's age.

"My uncle." She nodded and her eyes showed weariness. And sorrow. So much sorrow. How horrible was it to know a member of your family had tried to kill you? Twice.

Flynn was so close to his family, he couldn't even imagine. Tessa had been living with the worry of it for more than a decade. And now she had confirmation.

Without taking his eyes from hers, he gently took the gun from her, engaged the safety, and tucked it in a jacket pocket. Then he wrapped her in his arms as the rest headed down the stairs. "I was so damn scared, Tessa."

Her arms wrapped around his jacket. "Me too. But you're okay. You're all okay."

He leaned back and kissed her on the forehead and just breathed in her scent. Eventually the shaking would go away. "We're all okay. Come on. Let's head down with the others and get this wrapped up."

Tessa started to move but her gait was stiff. "Everyone's downstairs already. Will you let me carry you down?"

She stiffened under his hold, probably annoyed that her weakness was visible.

He tilted up her chin to look into her eyes. "It's only your legs that are weak, not you. You're so damn strong, Tessa."

146

Her smile was a bit wobbly, but it was a definite smile. Finally, she nodded, so Flynn scooped her up and hurried down the stairs. At the bottom, he slid her to her feet and snuck in another kiss. "Ready?"

He took her hand again, and realized it was wet. With blood. "You're hurt?"

He lifted her hand and saw a small trail of blood was dripping down her arm from a wound on her bicep. A gunshot wound. "That bastard shot you, Tessa."

"What?" But she frowned down at her arm.

This time he didn't ask. He lifted her into his arms and took her into the kitchen, calling for Mitch, who was a paramedic as well as a firefighter.

Tessa's dark blue sweater had hidden the blood but now he could see it oozing. He set her down on the counter and started hauling open drawers to find scissors.

"I'm fine, Flynn. It's not bad."

Blood was dripping on the counter. She wasn't fine.

Mitch rushed in and swore. "Gunshot?"

"I think so."

Bella had followed Mitch in and she gasped at the sight of Tessa bleeding. Mitch turned to her. "Grab the first aid kit for me." Then he pulled open a drawer Flynn hadn't reached yet and grabbed scissors.

Mitch smiled at Tessa. "Nice sweater, but it's going to be one sleeve short in a second." Before she could protest, his friend cut along the sleeve and eased it off her arm.

Rage filled Flynn when he saw the wound. If Tessa hadn't gripped his hand with her free one, he would have stormed into the room and ripped Kuzmetzov's head off his body. Instead, he forced himself to take deep breaths and to focus on Tessa.

Mitch took some of the cleaning fluid from the kit Bella brought into the room. He smiled wryly at Tessa. "I hate to be a cliché, but this is going to sting. Do you want something to bite down on?"

Tessa shook her head but her hand squeezed Flynn's. He hopped onto the counter beside her and cupped her head into his shoulder. "If you want to scream, do it. It's been a hell of a day and I might join in."

When Mitch applied the antiseptic, her body tensed, but she didn't make a sound.

"It's a through and through. Doesn't appear to be any damage to anything important and the bleeding is almost stopped. We'll get a doctor to check you over, but it should be fine. For now, I'm going to get it closed up and apply some gauze. Hang tight."

Still, Tessa didn't make a sound. He wondered if the events of the day had turned her numb and the pain would hit later.

Mitch turned to Bella. "Can you get her juice and some of that veggie-lentil dish Tansy made last night?"

"I'm fine."

Mitch grinned at her. "You're a hell of a lot better than fine, but this will help keep you from getting light-headed. We can't have your badass self fainting in front of the jackasses."

She managed a small smile at that and didn't argue when Flynn picked her up to set her on a chair. Bella pulled up another chair and shoved Flynn into it with his own food in front of him. "You look more light-headed than Tessa. Eat."

Tessa smiled and for that, Flynn would have eaten anything Bella put in front of him.

For a few minutes, no one spoke as they ate and Mitch finished dressing the wound and cleaned up the blood on the counter. Voices from the other room carried, but not clearly enough to hear the words.

Finally, Tessa sat back and nodded. "That helped. Thank you. What happens next?"

Flynn patted her hand and put her juice glass in front of her. "We called in a few agencies and law enforcement personnel. We'll probably wait until everyone gets here and figure out the next steps."

He looked up at the others. "Did anyone go help Troy bring the others in?"

Mitch nodded. "Joe, Graham, and Aisling went. The training ground's more than halfway to the sawmill, so they're going to head that way with the prisoners."

"I want to see him." Tessa's quiet voice had them all turning toward her.

Flynn took her hand. "Are you sure?" He wanted to wrap her in his arms and hide her away from the ugliness, but it was her call.

"I am." She stood and turned to the main room, but she didn't let go of his hand.

CHAPTER 20
Cops And Robbers

Tessa gripped Flynn's hand like the lifeline it was. She knew it had been her uncle on the stairs, but she had to ensure she wasn't imagining things and that she hadn't killed him. Had to show him she was still alive. And she wanted to know why he wanted her dead.

In the main room, four men were handcuffed and prone on the ground. Even though they were face-down, she knew which one was her uncle. As if he felt her attention, Karlo shifted and lifted his head. His gaze locked on hers and hate fairly sizzled across the room.

Tessa released Flynn's hand and moved closer. Karlo's gaze never left hers and his expression grew angrier the closer she came. Unsure if her legs would support her much longer, Tessa dropped into the chair nearest him. "Why?"

Karlo rolled his eyes. "Stupid bitch. You're nothing but trouble."

Tessa gripped the arm of the chair to stop her body from reacting. "I've never done anything to you."

He sneered at her. "You fucked it all up by simply existing. First your mama wanted to leave the family because of you. Wanted to hide you away. Then your father lied about his will. He left the money to you. Traitorous bastard. Thought we wouldn't find out."

"Money? This has all been about money? You've killed people for money?" Anger vibrated through her and she shoved to her feet. "You're pathetic."

She walked toward Flynn and then kept walking. She couldn't be in the same room with Karlo. He'd set her up to be killed and when that hadn't worked, had tried again. For money.

Tessa kept moving until she reached the workout room. Once again, she wished her body was up to using the treadmills to run away from her frustrations and hurts.

She hadn't been able to run since Karlo had blown up her house with her in it. Killing her father. Sending her to Wit Sec. Almost destroying her body. Had he also killed her mother?

A shudder ran through her, shaking her from head to toe.

"Hey." Flynn's soft voice drifted across the room. She heard him close the door, but she couldn't turn. All the energy she possessed was keeping her from shaking apart.

Flynn walked in front of her and then his strong body wrapped her in a hug so gentle, she couldn't hold herself together any more.

Sobs broke and he cradled her to him as she cried. For herself. For her mother. For her father. Even for her broken family. What had made them evil? What had broken them beyond repair?

Flynn held her gently, stroking her hair, and whispering soothing words to her. She managed to get herself under control and then she leaned into him, too worn to even lift her head. "Sorry about that."

He chuckled as he kissed her hair. "Nothing to be sorry about. You've been under unimaginable stress for over a decade. Letting it out isn't a bad thing."

His warmth and strength seeped into her and soothed her. "What happens next?"

He sighed into her hair. "The FBI team from Bedford should be here shortly. We'll coordinate with them and the other deputies Marcus called in. The men we've caught will all be taken to various detention centers and charged. Then there will be a million questions for all of us and a billion pounds of paperwork that has to be filled out."

Her body ached just thinking about it.

"But we'll get that arm checked out before you have to answer anything."

"Mitch fixed it up. I'm sure it's fine. I just want to get this over with."

He hugged her again. "I know. I wish I could make that happen for you."

That had her looking up. "I know you would. That wasn't a criticism, just a statement."

He kissed her forehead. "I know that, too."

"I called John Tynan, my US Marshal contact, earlier on. I'll have to call back and update him, although he was going to talk with the Houston FBI office. He was a little pissed I hadn't called him earlier, but when I told him the story, he mostly understood."

Someone knocked softly on the door and Flynn called for them to come in.

Sam opened the door and poked his head in. "How you doing, Tess?"

"I'm okay. Do you need us?"

He gave her a wry smile. "I could hold things off for a few minutes, but the teams are here and we want to get these guys off the property and locked up where they belong."

She nodded. "Okay."

When they walked to the door, Sam pulled her in for a hug of his own. "You did good, Tess. You all did. Now we can put these guys away and you can get on with your life."

His words shocked her and she couldn't do anything but hug him back. Then he turned and headed back to the main room.

Flynn tilted his head. "What is it? You look surprised."

She smiled at him. A real smile. "I hadn't thought it through yet. Do you think I can really live a normal life now? Do you think I can stop hiding?"

Flynn cupped her face and kissed her. "That's the plan."

"But my grandfather is still out there."

"Let's not borrow any trouble yet. We've got the man who tried to kill you back then and now. He's going to spend the rest of his life in prison. I don't think anyone is going to be stupid enough to try anything else."

Tessa nodded and walked with Flynn to start the process of dealing with the rest. Hope and dread warred within her.

If her grandfather kept sending people after her, it wasn't over. Not even close.

Would it ever be?

F lynn signed the last document and dropped the pen. The conference room in the Bedford FBI office was filled with his friends and other agents. Shanice Williams, the lead New Hampshire agent, had invited them to use her space as their temporary office while they dealt with the fallout of the attack on Midnight Lake.

It had taken more than twenty-four hours to get most of the details organized and wrapped up.

Kuzmetzov and the three men he'd brought up from Houston would be transported back with the US Marshals. The local thugs he'd hired would be kept locally. John Tynan, had been a great help in adding yet another law enforcement agency into the mix. This case could be a poster child for interagency cooperation.

Flynn would have to fly to Houston soon and finish out the case with his team. And then he'd tender his resignation and move on to Midnight Security full time. One night without Tessa in his bed had proven to him he was making the right decision.

Mitch and Bella had gone with her to the nearest medical center to get her arm checked out. Then they'd all given their statements to Marcus. Joe and Nico had come with Flynn to New Hampshire. The two-hour drive wasn't far, but still too far from home.

He pulled out his phone and texted Tessa. *How are you feeling?*

She sent back a laughing emoji. *Same as when you texted an hour ago. I'm fine. How are you doing?*

He grinned. *Missing you.*

Same.

We'll be wrapping up soon and hope to be back later this afternoon or evening.

Good news. Be safe.

You too.

He hesitated over adding, *Love you.* But he hadn't said it out loud to her face yet. He didn't want the first time he told her to be in a text. He wanted it to be when he had her in his arms, preferably in their bed.

His phone rang while he was thinking about getting Tessa naked. His boss. Clearing his mind, he answered. "Hey Janis."

"Word about Karlo Kuzmetzov's arrest has made its way to the locals down here."

"Already?"

"Never takes long enough. You'll want to be here sooner rather than later if you want to be in on the conversation with Grigor. We're going to move on the casino location tonight."

He couldn't miss this. "I'll be there. Once I have a flight, I'll text you the information."

A quick check had him swearing. The only flight out of the closest airport left in two hours. Time enough to get to there, but it was in the opposite direction of Midnight Lake. At least he'd grabbed his go-bag from the lodge before he'd left.

As soon as he was in the car, he called Tessa. "I'm sorry, honey. I've got to go to Houston. I'm heading to the Manchester airport and I'm on the next plane."

"Why do you have to go? What's wrong? Did Karlo escape?"

He hadn't meant to scare her. "Sorry. It's not that kind of emergency. My boss called and it appears Grigor Pavic has heard the news. My team will mobilize soon and I need to be there."

There was a pause and Flynn wished he'd been able to make a video call. He wanted to see her face, see what she was thinking.

"Okay. Make sure you're safe."

He nodded even though she couldn't see him. "I will." His phone beeped and he looked to see it was Janis. "Sorry, Tessa. My boss is on the line. Gotta go. I'll talk to you when I can."

"Goodbye, Flynn." Her sad tone had him wishing he could ignore his boss, but that was never a smart move. Flynn took the call and then spent his remaining time on the drive and then on the plane setting up the op. It was going to be a long night. But it would be a huge step toward closing up his last FBI case.

As long as nothing went sideways.

CHAPTER 21

Top Secret

Tessa slipped on her backpack and picked up her walking cane. Pride was going to have to take a back seat to practicality. She would only use the cane when necessary, but she figured the trip was going to be difficult enough. She'd take all the support she could get.

On the main floor of the lodge, she found Sam and Tansy in the kitchen, preparing pasta and a sauce that smelled like onions, garlic, and all things comforting. Both looked up and Sam's eyes immediately narrowed. "What's going on? Why are you leaving? Where are you going?"

Tansy patted Sam's arm but kept her gaze on Tessa. "What's wrong?"

She smiled at these two amazing people. "You two are the best. I'm not leaving permanently. I'll be back in a few days."

Sam frowned. "You're going to Houston."

Tansy gasped. "No. It's not safe for you there."

Her own smile was a little wobbly. "It'll be fine. Karlo and his buddies are in jail. By now, my grandfather knows I'm alive. If I'm going to live without looking over my shoulder every moment, I need to see him. To find out how to end this."

Tansy pulled off her apron. "I'll go with you."

Sam moved to wash his hands at the sink. "We both will."

Tessa's eyes misted. "Thank you. Both of you. You really are the best people I know. But my flight is soon and I need to leave now. I'm hoping I can take the golf cart to the sawmill."

Sam turned off the stove. "We'll get you to your car."

Throughout the drive to the car, her friends continued to try to talk her into letting them go along, but she stood firm. "There are so many law enforcement people watching my grandfather right now. It's the perfect time to talk to him."

Sam glanced at her. "Does Flynn know you're going?"

She shook her head. "Not yet. He's on his own flight right now. I'll let him know when I get there."

After hugs from Tansy and terse advice from Sam on how to stay alert and safe, Tessa got in her car and drove to Burlington to catch her flight. Part of her wanted to shout at them to jump in and come along, but it was time to stop putting other people in danger and be a grownup. With Karlo in jail, there was no immediate danger. She would deal with her grandfather and keep the target well away from her friends.

By the time she touched down in Houston, it was late, and she was a bouncy ball of nerves. She'd changed her mind about her plan a dozen times.

Still, she wanted a future and she figured the best way to create that was to speak with her grandfather in person. She'd never had much contact with him. Her memories were mostly of awkward holiday dinners where she'd been under strict instruction to not speak unless someone asked her a direct question. Escaping the table as early as possible had been her goal and she wasn't sure she'd ever had a private moment with the man.

From her recent research, she'd found her grandfather had moved to the most expensive area of Houston and away from where he managed his deals. If she grabbed a cab and headed to his place in the River Oaks district now, she wouldn't arrive until after midnight. Part of her wanted to go anyway. Get it over with. But she probably wouldn't be let in the door arriving at that time of night.

She pulled out her phone and powered it up. It had been so long since she'd left Midnight Lake and she needed contact with Flynn. She'd sent him a text before she'd boarded, but had turned it off for the flight.

After she cleared security and was in the main terminal, she checked the phone and found multiple notifications. She ignored them and called his number. If he was sleeping or busy, she would leave a message, but hearing his voice was a priority.

"Tessa. You called."

That made her smile. "Of course."

He sighed into the phone. "I thought you were going off grid on a solo mission."

She gnawed at her lower lip. "I hate to admit that I thought about it, but I couldn't do it. I want to have the life we're building at Midnight Lake and I can't do that if I'm not honest with you. I love you, Flynn." The words flew out before she could think about them.

"I'm very glad to hear that."

But the voice wasn't coming from the phone which had disconnected. She turned to find Flynn approaching and no one had ever looked better.

She grinned then he cupped her face and kissed her. She dropped her walking cane and wrapped her arms around him while she kissed him back with everything she had. With him, she didn't need any other support.

Flynn pulled back and his eyes locked on hers. "I love you, too, Tessa. So damn much. I was waiting for the perfect time to say it, but you're right. We need to be honest. And the truth is I love you."

Then they were kissing again, in the middle of the airport. Maybe not the most romantic place for declarations, but it was perfect.

Joy filled her up and she felt like she could take on any and all challenges with this man at her side.

Eventually, Flynn pulled back again and then hugged her. Those big strong arms were everything she needed. When he released her, he bent to pick up the cane she'd dropped. He handed it to her while slipping her backpack off her back. "Let me take this."

Because it was Flynn, she relinquished the weight without feeling weird or weak. Grinning, he took her hand and tugged her towards the door. "My Jeep's this way."

It wasn't long before they were in the Jeep and driving away. She was glad she didn't have to navigate. She wasn't familiar with this part of Houston, and her nerves were bouncing at being back in Texas. So close to where her life had changed forever.

Houston wasn't the way it was in her memory. The highways were wider and faster. Flynn was traveling at the speed limit, but vehicles zipped by them like they were standing still. She hadn't seen a single green space either. It was concrete everywhere she looked.

As if reading her thoughts, Flynn reached over and squeezed her hand. "Doing okay? How's it feel being here?"

"Terrifying. Wonderful. Weird."

He laughed. "That probably covers it. My condo is close to the office, so we won't be going near familiar territory today. But we can tomorrow if you'd like."

She leaned her head back to consider that. "I don't know. And I didn't come for a vacation. I want to go to see my grandfather tomorrow. I need to talk to him."

Flynn's hand flinched in hers. "I knew you were going to say that, but I don't like it." Traffic was busy, so he took his hand back to put on the wheel.

"I can't say I like it much either, but I feel like it's the right thing to do. I don't want to go back into hiding and this is my best shot at doing that."

Flynn nodded. "I'd like to go with you."

No demand. No takeover. But not a question either. "I'd like that, too."

Flynn pulled into his condo's garage with a sense of rightness. Coming home with Tessa beside him.

He'd kept his emotions under a tight leash since he'd spotted her in the airport, since hearing she loved him back. Those emotions were growling for release and he wanted her in his bed, but he knew she might not be up to it. "How are your legs after being on a plane for so long?"

She shrugged as she got out of the Jeep. "A little stiff. Nothing major."

He grabbed her bag and took her hand. "I've got things I have to tell you, but I can't think of anything except that you love me back."

Tessa's eyes twinkled. "Same."

He opened the door to the mudroom and headed to the front hall. "Let's skip the tour and the conversation. Ready?"

"With you? For anything."

Hell. Her words made him feel like a conquering hero who'd vanquished the hordes of evil-doers. Tossing her bag over his shoulder, he scooped her up in his arms and sprinted up to the third floor and into his bedroom. He didn't stop there but moved straight into the bathroom with its amazing shower. He finally set her on her feet and realized she'd undone all the buttons on his shirt and her hands were working on his belt buckle.

"I like the way you think."

She laughed. "Then help me out here, cowboy."

He followed orders until there were no more barriers between them. He grabbed a condom from the drawer and tossed it into the shower and cranked the water.

Then he let his hands touch. He wanted to touch her everywhere at once. From her head to her toes. Over her scars and happy spots.

In the shower, he used his body wash to massage her skin and ease the aches. And if he happened to spend more time on her breasts, he wasn't apologizing for it. Especially when she was so responsive to his touch.

When he couldn't stand it anymore, he grabbed the condom and sheathed himself. He boosted her up and held her poised just above him. "Say it, Tessa. Say it again."

"I love you, Flynn."

He lowered her as she said the words and they both groaned when he was fully seated inside her.

Tessa arched backward, pushing the contact even deeper.

When he started to move, she used her fingers to trail over his abs, his chest, his shoulders, and into his hair. Everywhere she touched, she left fireworks.

He reached between them and in only moments sent her shuddering over the edge. His name flew from her lips like a prayer.

He kept touching, kept pumping as she drifted back to awareness. Her lashes flickered up and she smiled at him. "I love you, Flynn."

Her words had him thrusting faster, harder.

She repeated her words, the phrase becoming a chant.

When she flew again, he thrust twice more, then exploded into her.

Drawing in gulps of air, he kept a hold of her while they recovered. "You okay to stand?"

She laughed and nodded. "I'm good. You?"

He laughed as he cleaned up the condom and they rinsed off. "I'm good. Now maybe I can concentrate on something other than ripping your clothes off."

He grabbed a towel and wrapped it around her, pulling her in for another kiss. "I doubt I'll ever stop wanting to do that, though."

"Sounds good to me."

Laughing they dried off and Flynn forced himself to think about Pavic. "A lot has happened in the case since we left Midnight Lake. I'm going to have to leave in a couple of minutes."

"What? It's the middle of the night. Why? What's happening?"

He took her shaking hands and kissed her. "It's okay. I'll tell you while I get dressed."

He moved into his bedroom and pulled out clothes suitable for a night mission. All black. "We've had eyes on the location of the illegal casino you picked out. We're going in tonight to break it up and take it down."

She sat on the edge of the bed and he had to simply stop and enjoy the picture of her wrapped in his towel, sitting on his bed.

"Will my grandfather be there?"

"Doubtful. We don't have any confirmed sightings of him going in or being in the area at all. In fact, no one's had eyes on him since the attack back at home."

Home. This condo should be his home. Even though he'd been thinking possessively of Tessa in his space, his mind had already accepted that Houston was his past. His future was up north with Tessa.

"So he could be at home or in the casino?"

He nodded. "Could be either, or somewhere else entirely. My gut says he's at home. There's no reason to believe he's got a living space in the casino. He's moved away from his operations. He's separating himself from them, maybe passing things on to Karlo."

Tessa stood and grabbed her bag, pulled out a pair of jeans and a long-sleeved tee.

"What are you doing?"

"I'm coming with you. I didn't come all the way here to be left behind."

He found her stubborn eyes directly on his. "It's an FBI op, Tessa. No civilians allowed."

She shrugged but continued dressing.

He put on his holster and strapped his backup weapon to his ankle. "We can go to see your grandfather tomorrow. I have to be with my team on this."

He'd already scooted out of the operation because Sam had called to tell him Tessa's flight information.

She nodded. "We can. But I'm still going with you. I'm not going to run into the casino and make a mess of things. I'll stay somewhere safe, but I need to be part of this."

His boss was going to chew his ass. She might be glad when he tendered that resignation.

CHAPTER 22
Family Business

Tessa was relieved Flynn hadn't tried to force her to stay behind. She'd have taken a cab down to the area if she'd had to, but it was better to be with him, to not do anything behind his back. He wasn't thrilled she wanted to ride along, but he'd let her.

During the ride, he spent most of the time on the phone with his team while she'd watched the Christmas lights strung up across the city. He'd explained she'd been with him right away so the conversation had probably been careful on both ends. She hoped he wasn't going to be in trouble because she'd insisted on tagging along.

After a fifteen minute drive, he pulled into a parking garage and found a spot near the elevator. She didn't ask any questions, especially once they were out of the car. They moved into the elevator, his hand on the small of her back, making her feel safe and loved.

The thought had her smiling. He loved her. That might be the most amazing feeling in the world. If only she could travel back in time to tell the girl waking up alone and terrified in the hospital that one day Flynn Walker would be in love with her. That would have made doing all that physical therapy so much easier.

On the eighth floor, they got out and Tessa realized they were in a hotel. Flynn took out a key card and ushered her into the room ahead of him.

They walked into the sitting room of a large suite. She could see a bedroom beyond and a bathroom to the side. Eight agents worked at various tables and desks. Most wore headsets and sat at computers. Files and papers covered the horizontal spaces. The hum of data analysis in action helped calm her nerves. These were her people.

A tall, mixed-race woman stood and approached them. "Agent Walker." Her voice carried an Arctic breeze.

Flynn nodded his greeting. "Special Agent Jenkins, I'd like you to meet Tessa Flores."

The woman didn't offer to shake her hand, so Tessa kept hers clasped together. "Nice to meet you."

"As Special Agent Walker isn't in the habit of toting civilians along on investigations, I assume you insisted on being here. Why?"

Tessa gathered all her nerves and squeezed her hands so her voice wouldn't shake. "This entire mess involves my family. I've been in hiding since I was seventeen. I don't want to hide anymore. The only way to do that is to stop the Pavic family from trying to kill me. To do that, I need to speak with my grandfather. I'm willing to wait until after you finish your plans for the night before contacting him."

For a heartbeat, Tessa wondered if she'd been rude, if she'd crossed a line. Jenkins maintained eye contact for a count of five before nodding with a small smile. She offered her hand. "Nice to meet you, Miss Flores. I hear from Shanice Williams that you're a whiz at data analysis."

Too surprised to speak, Tessa nodded.

Jenkins pointed across the room. "The mobile team is going to move out, and you're going to stay here and help at this end. If you leave, that's up to you, but I don't want you interfering at the casino site. Leave that to us so that you don't endanger anyone." She sent a pointed look at Flynn. "Or that you don't distract anyone from doing their job. I'd hate to lose an agent tonight because you needed closure."

"I won't interfere. But I want your word that I'll have a chance to speak with my grandfather if he's at the casino tonight."

Jenkins raised an eyebrow but finally nodded. "We don't have any intel that he's there, but if we bring him into custody, you'll have your chance." Then the formidable woman moved toward the door.

Tessa blew out a breath and smiled at Flynn. He grinned back. "Nicely done. I'll be back as soon as I can."

Tessa grabbed his hand. "Be safe."

"That's the plan." Then he kissed her quickly and followed his boss out the door.

F lynn had missed the mission briefing when he'd taken off to the airport to meet Tessa, so he wasn't part of the team that would be going inside the casino. While he preferred to be in the midst of the action, he wouldn't have traded the past couple of hours for anything.

He found himself in the support van with Jenkins and a couple of other agents, monitoring communications and guiding the op. At least his boss hadn't kicked him out completely. Tessa had probably helped. Janis respected forthrightness.

Their agents were scattered in various locations, watching and waiting for their cues. Once everyone was set, Agents Lopez and Chu headed toward what they believed was the club entrance.

Dressed in the very best the wardrobe department had to offer, the two looked every bit like a wealthy couple ready to get a little drunk and lose a lot of money.

In real life, Lopez was a gentle giant and Chu a martial arts expert. They played the couple vibe well and had been used in several assignments. The combination of flirt and charm never failed to get them into any place they wanted.

Through the mic, he heard Chu using her sultry voice on the bouncer and Lopez subtly offering his hand, with bribe securely hidden.

Sure enough, in less than twenty seconds, they were inside the back door of the building and up the private elevator to the casino that was indeed on the hidden floor behind the ballroom.

The agents kept their conversation casual as they *oohed* and *aahed* over the setup, letting their team know the layout of the place and the placement of security cameras and personnel. No one listening would hear anything unusual because they'd created their own code for sharing information.

One of the several screens in front of Flynn showed the blueprints of the building, but he had to imagine the layout of the casino itself. Another agent tapped him on the shoulder and placed a tablet she'd been working on at his elbow. She'd used the information from Chu and Lopez to sketch out the actual casino layout. He grinned at her. "That's amazing, Hassan. Exactly what we need. Thanks."

With the new map, he and Jenkins fine-tuned the strategy and redirected agents with new placements and timing.

Chu's pouty voice came through the mic. "I don't see any of our friends here, honey. Do you think they found another club for tonight?"

That meant neither of them had spotted Grigor Pavic or any of his top tier. Flynn couldn't decide if that was good or bad news. For the op, it would have been better to catch the man running the place. For Tessa, it was better if he wasn't there.

His hopes for Tessa overrode his hopes for the op which was another sign he was ready to move on from this job.

Using their prearranged codes, Chu alerted the team of the office location and announced they were in position. Jenkins opened her mic to all operatives and counted down from five. The agents on the outside moved in while Chu and Lopez burst into the office and secured that section.

It was over in about ninety seconds with no shots fired and no injuries. He, Jenkins, and the others moved in to separate those running the casino from the gamblers.

He recognized several politicians and big name celebrities who were pissed about being caught in an illegal place and were whining for lawyers. Ignoring them, he moved to the office where he found a few familiar faces from their research. People Tessa has guessed these people were third-tier employees working for her grandfather. The woman was dead-on with her analysis.

Houston PD arrived to assist with interviewing and interrogating, but it was still hours before they wrapped up the onsite work.

Eventually, he and Jenkins stood on the sidewalk watching the last of those arrested being driven away. His boss turned to him, smiling. "A nice bit of work for your last op as a Special Agent."

Flynn stared at her. Was she firing him?

For a few moments she simply stared at him, then she smirked. "Did you think I couldn't see how in love you are with your data analyst? The gossip vine tells me you've got a foothold in a security business up north. You planning on doing that full time?"

He laughed and shook his head. "I've barely said a word about Midnight Security and absolutely nothing about moving on."

Jenkins rolled her eyes dramatically. "Superior Special Agent skills here, Walker. Plus, I've got eyes and ears in more places than you'll ever know. So, what's the plan?"

Flynn nodded. "This case has been my bailiwick. It's the reason I joined the FBI. After we wrap this up and Tessa gets her chance to speak with Grigor, I'm going to move on to Midnight Security."

Jenkins nodded. "I hate to lose you, but this job isn't always a long-term one. If you ever need anything, be sure to reach out."

He shook her hand. "And if you need someone on the outside, let me know if I can help."

"Will do. Now, let's go back to the hotel and see what the team has figured out and concluded. Then, take your Tessa over to Pavic's place in River Oaks and see if you can wrap this up."

"River Oaks?" That neighborhood had to be one of the most expensive in Texas.

"Nothing but the best for our friend Pavic."

Hopefully that meant the man had enough and would be willing to take the target off Tessa's back.

CHAPTER 23
All In The Family

Even though she was surrounded by agents and lost in the data analysis, Tessa felt the air change and knew Flynn had walked into the hotel suite. Either she was beyond exhausted and imagining things or she was so in love that she was attuned to his presence.

She looked up to find his gaze locked on hers from where he stood by the door. She'd known there were no injuries, but seeing him whole and grinning at her was the best feeling.

Unable to help herself, she rose and met him halfway across the room. She wrapped her arms around him. "I'm so glad you're safe."

He kissed her hair and squeezed her back. "Right back atcha."

Not wanting to embarrass him in front of his team, she stepped back. He took her hand as he moved back to where his boss stood.

Janis Jenkins studied her. "How do you feel about wearing a wire when you meet with your grandfather?"

The question stumped her for a moment. She'd never thought of that. "Why?"

"We'd like the conversation on tape, but only with your permission."

Over the hours since the raid at the casino, the agents had told her there'd been nothing at the casino to implicate Grigor Pavic, even though they had all believed he was involved. The team wanted information about his operations, but that part wasn't why Tessa wanted to speak with him.

She thought over the pros and cons of wearing the wire and finally shook her head. "I'm sorry. I don't think I can do that. Not this time. If I meet with him a second time, I'll consider it again. I want honest answers from him and I can't demand that if I'm not being honest myself."

Jenkins frowned but nodded. "I can't say I'm not disappointed, but I understand."

Tessa looked at Flynn. "But I'd like Flynn to go with me."

He smiled. "You couldn't stop me from going."

Jenkins rolled her eyes. "When do you plan to go see him?"

Tessa hadn't expected all these questions. Her mind was gritty from staying up all night but she knew she wouldn't be able to sleep until she'd seen her grandfather. "Now."

Flynn studied her for a moment and then nodded. "Okay. We might as well keep going. Get it done before we need to crash. You sure you're up for this?"

She nodded. "As ready as I'll ever be." Which wasn't saying a lot.

Once they were in Flynn's Jeep, he turned to her. "What are you thinking?"

That made her laugh. "I'm not even sure. So many pieces of data are whirling through my brain. No one found anything connecting Grigor to the casino. There were plenty of Karlo connections, but nothing with my grandfather. Is it possible that there's nothing to find?"

"You think Karlo was running this under his nose and Pavic didn't know anything about it? That doesn't seem likely."

Not when he said it like that. "I know. The agents and I couldn't make sense of it either. There was all kinds of earlier evidence. That's how I found the location in the first place. But nothing recent."

"You think he's maybe passed on the business?"

She shrugged. "Maybe? My gut says it's Karlo's business now and the information is all pointing at him." Would that be good news or bad?

Flynn ran his hand under her hair to rub the back of her neck. "It's okay to not be sure. Most police work is asking questions, making theories, proving and disproving them. And research. Lots and lots of research. We'll figure this out."

Then he kissed her. Lightly at first, but it deepened in a heartbeat.

When he pulled back into his seat, he pointed a finger at her. "You, Tessa Flores, are a dangerous woman. You ready to do this?"

Rubbing her fingers over her lips, she smiled and nodded. If anyone was dangerous, it was the sexy rodeo star turned FBI agent sitting next to her.

Dangerous in the very best way.

Flynn started the Jeep and drove out of the parking garage and to the west. The sun was up and people were heading to their jobs, making traffic its usual nightmare. That eased when they moved into residential areas, each better off than the last.

She'd grown up in houses like the ones around her and she wondered how many were filled with sad stories. They might be beautiful houses but were they homes?

The houses got bigger and the manicured lawns fancier. Tessa's nerves grew right along with them. It seemed like only moments before Flynn turned down a quiet street with stone fences and gates surrounding most of the houses.

When Flynn turned into the drive, they found it locked with a buzzer system. Tessa blew out a breath and nodded.

Flynn pressed the buzzer. A man's voice responded. "Yes." Not even a question, more of a statement.

When Flynn opened his mouth to speak, she squeezed his arm and leaned closer to the window. "This is Tessa Flores. I'm here to speak with my grandfather."

There was no response. She wondered if she should have used her former name, but it didn't fit anymore. She wasn't Catalina Blanco, hadn't been for a very long time. After all that had happened over the past week, it seemed impossible Grigor wouldn't know the name she now used.

Finally, the voice responded. "Park in front of the steps. Be prepared for a security check."

The gate slid soundlessly open and Flynn drove through. They drove through a parklike lawn until the trees opened up to show an enormous house. White. Cold. She'd bet this house wasn't a home either.

Three men waited. Two at the bottom of the stairs, one at the top. All tall, strong, and armed.

Flynn squeezed her hand as he turned off the engine. "We've got this. Show how strong you are. Wait until I open your door." Then he leaned over and kissed her quickly.

She felt silly sitting in the car while he got out. He made eye contact with all the men while he walked easily around the hood and to her door. He opened it and smiled at her while he held out his hand to her.

She took it, blew out a breath, and stood. They turned and looked at the men. They all wore blank faces and one stepped forward. "Any weapons?"

They both shook their heads, but Flynn spoke. "My gun is in the glove compartment. It's locked."

"I need to pat you down."

Flynn stepped forward and stood with his arms to the side and an open stance. When the man was done, he turned to Tessa. She copied Flynn's stance, glad she was wearing jeans and not a dress. The man was quick, like a pat-down at the airport. Nothing invasive or creepy.

The inane thought that at least her grandfather didn't hire lecherous thugs almost made her smile. Almost.

"Follow me. Do not touch anything or anyone."

Okay then.

Flynn took her hand again and they followed the man into the big, cold house.

F lynn had walked through his share of multi-million dollar homes in his years as an agent, and this one was near the top of the scale. Lots of art and rugs that probably each cost more than he'd make in his lifetime.

And he'd trade it all for the room he shared at Midnight Lake with

Tessa. Nothing here screamed home or family. Had Tessa's home been like this? Cold and without a soul?

He wondered again at how she'd turned out to be such an amazing woman. She'd had so few role models, but she'd succeeded in overcoming her past.

No wonder he was head over spurs in love with her. He lifted their joined hands and kissed her fingers. She looked at him, eyes wide.

He grinned at her. "Just remembering why I love you so damn much. You're amazing."

Her eyes softened and she reached up on her toes to press a kiss to his lips. "So are you."

The two guards who remained in the foyer with them didn't react to their exchange, but kept their attention firmly on them in case they'd snuck in a grenade or poison.

The head guard returned from down a hallway. "This way."

They followed him but didn't get much more of a view of the rest of the house. The man stopped at the first door and opened it, preceding them in to protect anyone inside from a potential threat. The other two followed a few feet behind.

The room was an office with a huge wooden desk that was designed to make the occupant the center of attention. Not a speck of dust would dare rest on the polished surface that held nothing. No evidence to be found if nothing was on display. Not that Flynn had expected the man to leave out incriminating documents.

Behind the desk, Grigor Pavic rose but didn't extend his hand. He remained behind the desk, in front of the window. A typical power position used by those wanting to intimidate. It always made Flynn roll his eyes.

The man stood about six feet tall, styled steel grey hair, tailored suit that rivaled the rugs for cost. His hard eyes softened slightly as he stared at Tessa.

"You're so much like her." His whispered words seemed to be pulled reluctantly from his lips.

Without looking away from his granddaughter, he spoke to his guards. "Leave us."

"Sir?"

At that, his icy gaze moved to the guard who'd dared question him. "I hardly think my granddaughter and Agent Walker are on a suicide mission to kill me. Leave us."

Flynn wasn't surprised Pavic knew his identity. The man probably had eyes and ears throughout Houston. He also wasn't surprised when the door closed behind them a moment later. If these guards wanted to keep their jobs, they'd be smart not to question any orders.

"Catalina. Tessa. Which name do you prefer?"

Flynn heard Tessa blow out a soft breath and she held his hand in a death grip, but she kept her voice steady. "I'm Tessa now. Tessa Flores. I've had to leave Catalina behind."

Pavic nodded. "Is Flores an allusion to your mother's name?"

"In part. It's also a tribute to a man who treated me like a daughter."

That brought a slight frown to Pavic's face. Probably trying to figure out who Tessa meant. Flynn didn't have to wonder. Tessa had only spent one day at his ranch, had only met his dad that one time. Marty Walker had made a hell of an impact and Flynn couldn't be prouder.

Tessa's voice was soft when she spoke. "Did you order Karlo to kill her? My mother? Your daughter?"

Pavic's face froze and his frown deepened. "No."

"Did you order him to kill me?" Her voice hadn't weakened, her eye contact never wavered.

"No." Pavic's gaze stayed steady as well and Flynn believed him. After a few moments, he closed his eyes briefly. Flynn wouldn't say his stance relaxed, but it softened.

Pavic moved from the desk to a bookshelf and took down a framed photo. He rounded the desk and approached, then offered the photo to Tessa.

"Mama?" Her voice was soft and laden with tears.

Pavic cleared his throat and his voice was thick as well. "Your mama. My Rosa. My beautiful Rosa. You believe Karlo killed her?"

Tessa's head whipped up. "Yes. He didn't say it outright, but he said I'd messed up everything by being born. That my mother wanted to take me away and that my father hadn't written a will to leave everything to the family. He implied he killed them both."

Pavic's body language hardened again and his eyes turned to granite.

This was the man who'd run an organized outfit for decades. "I see." Flynn figured Karlo was going to be safer in jail than outside of it.

Pavic paced away and looked out a window for a long moment. When he turned again, his eyes were still angry, but the man tempered his voice for his granddaughter. "I have never been a threat to you. I will never be a threat to you. Go and live your life, Tessa. Live without fear."

Then Pavic turned to Flynn. "You will make sure she remains safe."

It wasn't a question, but Flynn answered it anyway. "With my last breath."

Pavic nodded. "You will not always be alone in that duty."

Well, hell, Flynn hadn't expected an offer of mob protection.

Pavic turned back to Tessa. "I am glad you had the courage to come, but it is best you do not return. Live well, Catalina. Live well."

Pavic pressed a button on the side of his desk and the door behind them immediately opened. The three guards entered. "See our guests out."

Tessa offered the frame back, but Pavic shook his head. "Keep it and remember your mama loved you."

Then he turned and walked behind his desk. The guards ushered them outside and to the car. The gate opened to let them out and then closed immediately behind them.

Neither of them spoke as Flynn drove to his condo. Inside the garage, he turned off the Jeep and angled to see Tessa. She stared straight ahead and gripped the frame like a lifeline.

Flynn moved around the Jeep, opened her door and unbuckled her seatbelt. She startled and looked up at him, eyes full of unshed tears.

Flynn scooped her up and moved through the house into the living room. He sat on the couch and cradled her in his arms. "Tell me what you're feeling."

Tessa snuggled in and held out the photo. "I've never seen a photo of my mom before."

That jolted Flynn. Her youth had been so cold. "I'm glad you have it now."

She held out the photo and he got a look at it. A woman with Tessa's curls and glowing smile held a baby girl—Tessa—in her arms.

Rosa sat on a porch swing with flowers growing in pots all around her. "You can feel how happy she is."

Tessa nodded. "I never knew if she wanted me. I pretended she did. Pretended she had been thrilled to be a mom and had been devastated to leave me behind when she died."

He kissed her hair and his own voice was shaky when he spoke. "Now you know those things are true. She loved you. I think your grandfather did, too."

She nodded. "It was so strange to see him again. He looked older, tired. At times just as hard and cold as I remember, but there was something more there, too."

Flynn touched the photo. "Love. There was love there, too. Maybe some regret along with it." And a shit-ton of anger directed at Karlo.

"So, I didn't imagine it?"

"Not unless I did, too. I don't think he had a clue that Karlo was behind your mother's death. Or the explosion at your house."

She nodded. "It's weird to feel such relief at that. Not everyone hated me. He didn't want me dead."

Flynn squeezed her closer. "He didn't. He doesn't. You're free from it all, Tessa. You did it."

When she looked up at him, tears tracked down her cheeks, but she smiled at him. "We did it. I wouldn't be free without you. I love you."

"I love you too, Tessa." And while he knew she would have figured her way into the future without him, he was damn glad they'd done it together.

CHAPTER 24
Cowboy Christmas

T he next morning, Tessa sat in Flynn's Jeep and worked to keep her breathing normal. She'd asked him to take her back to the street where she'd grown up and she wasn't going to change her mind. She wanted to come full circle, to see what had happened to the home where she'd lived. Been blown up in.

Flynn's soft voice reached her ears. "We don't have to do this. You have nothing to prove. You survived a crappy childhood, a horrific attack, and you're successful in every way imaginable."

His words warmed her even though she wasn't sure he was right. "I don't know about that, but I want to do this. I don't want to be scared of the past anymore. Maybe seeing will help me believe it's over."

"We're almost there."

She nodded. "Can you go slowly?"

He grinned mischievously. "I can go slowly, very slowly, while I drive you over the edge. But for this, as long as there's no traffic behind me."

A laugh burst out of her. He could always make her laugh. Some of the tension ebbed with the laugh and she studied the neighborhood. A few houses had been updated, but the feel was the same. Snotball City.

When Flynn turned onto the street where she'd lived, he slowed again, then pulled over to the side. He slid the Jeep into park and turned to her. "Okay?"

She nodded. "I never googled the past, not even once. I don't know if the house was wholly destroyed. If someone rebuilt it or if it was bull-dozed for something new."

He squeezed her hand. "There wasn't much left. It was taken down and the property was empty for a while. Eventually another house was built and then put up for sale. I'm assuming that was Grigor at work, but I don't know."

Relief surged through her that she wouldn't have to see the dregs of a house that had been broken as badly as she had been. "I wonder where Mrs. O ended up."

Their cook had been Tessa's favorite person growing up. Brisk and efficient but always with a twinkle in her eye and a cookie to pass along. Tessa hadn't been allowed to mingle with the staff, but Mrs. O had been unfailingly kind and calm.

"That I don't know, but I bet we can find out. I have a connection at the FBI."

That elicited another chuckle. She leaned over the console and kissed him. "Thanks. I'm okay now. Let's have a look."

Seeing another house where hers had once sat ended up being anti-climatic. She'd expected big emotions and memories. Nothing. The new home didn't look anything like her old one, but had the same cold appearance. Dignified with no emotion behind it. It only took moments before she was ready to move on.

Flynn smiled. "Want to check out the school?"

She nodded immediately and Flynn drove the route her school bus had taken, bringing good memories. She'd always enjoyed learning. While the people part had been more of a challenge, the classes had been interesting. Soon they sat outside Circle Strong High School.

The memories were even better here. Most of those revolved around Flynn and math class. "I'm not sure I would have even dreamed it was possible to have a future with you."

He picked up her hand and kissed it. "Me neither. I thought you were too smart for me. Thought you'd find a billionaire to whisk you off to see the wonders of the world."

That made her laugh. "Well, he may not be a billionaire, but the guy I love has helped me to see the real wonders of the world."

He smiled and then kissed her again. The passion rose and filled the car. Someone tooted their horn and cheered as they drove by.

Tessa pulled back, laughing. "Caught making out in the parking lot. I never imagined reaching that level of cool."

Flynn kissed her quickly again before putting the Jeep in gear. "Ready for one more side trip?"

She nodded. She'd go on any number of side trips with this man.

Within a minute, she realized he was heading to his parents' ranch. He'd called them earlier and told them the whole story. Tessa had hidden out on another level of his condo, not wanting to make the conversation awkward and wanting them to be able to speak freely.

She'd known he would want to go to visit them if he was in the area, but she hadn't thought it through more than that.

Would they think she'd abandoned their son by hiding out in Wit Sec? Would they blame her because Flynn had left the rodeo and ranching life to join the FBI?

Would they even remember her? That day had been so special to her, but it was probably just another day for them with another of Flynn's friends.

Her heart rate picked up as she saw the entry to Walker Ranch. The Christmas lights strung along the sign reminded her the holiday was only a few days away, another thing she didn't know much about.

Marty and Shelley Walker were the kindest people she'd known. She could only hope that hadn't changed.

Flynn knew Tessa was nervous, just as he knew she needn't be worried. His parents were thrilled to hear she was alive and well. Thrilled to hear he was in love.

But Tessa wouldn't truly believe any of that until she'd experienced it for herself. She'd had no one like his folks growing up. No one at her back, no one ready to listen, no one with open arms.

The security cameras at the gate would have alerted his parents to their arrival, so he wasn't surprised to find them waiting on the front porch, which was covered with poinsettias and wreath. His brothers Beau and Morgan were there too.

His mom practically bounced in place, his dad's arm around her shoulders the only thing anchoring her to the wood beneath her feet. All four were grinning and he'd barely parked the Jeep when his mom threw open Tessa's door. He reached over to pop her seatbelt open, knowing his mom was about to haul her out.

Sure enough, in seconds, Tessa was surrounded by his mom. His dad had the two of them wrapped up in his powerful arms. Both brothers were grinning and came around to hug Flynn.

"The FBI gig making you soft yet?" Beau threw a punch at Flynn's gut, but pulled it at the last second.

"Still tough enough to take you down anytime."

Morgan tapped his mom on the shoulder. "Let the girl breathe, Ma. The rest of us want in on the hugs, too."

First one brother, then the other hugged Tessa, both telling her how glad they were to see her.

Beau grinned. "You're the only girl Flynn brought around who made him goofy. Hope you're still keeping him off-balance."

Morgan nodded. "Remember when she came out for the day? All he could talk about was how much fun he'd had. The perma-smile stuck on his face was hilarious."

Beau slapped Flynn on the back. "We even tricked him into mucking out the stalls for a week because he was so starry-eyed."

The ridiculous banter kept going as they moved a wide-eyed Tessa up the stairs and through the door. They kept moving into the kitchen, the heart of the farmhouse. Christmas had taken over here as well, with a small tree standing in the corner and his mom's reindeer collection on full display on every surface.

The big dining room table was set for six and he drooled at the scents filling the kitchen. "You made pies?"

His mom rolled her eyes. "Of course I made pies. I remember how your girl liked them. Told me she'd never tasted better."

Tessa finally spoke, her voice thick with emotion. "You remember? I've still never tasted better."

His mom wrapped her in another hug. "Of course we remember. You're a special young lady and you were so polite and excited to see how a ranch operated. A little scared of the horses, but up you went anyway."

Then his mom cupped Tessa's face and her tone changed to serious. "I'm so sorry for all you've been through, for all you've lost. We all are. But this is a time for celebration and we're not going to allow sad memories to intrude today. We can do that another time, but today is for happy."

She kissed both of Tessa's cheeks, then grinned. "Now, tell me if my boy's been treating you well. If not, there are always stables that need mucking out."

"Mom."

Tessa's eyes shone with moisture as she laughed. "You raised him well. He's a perfect gentleman and everything a girl could want."

Beau and Morgan groaned while his mom puffed up. Flynn was grinning as his dad slapped him on the shoulder with a grin.

His mom wiped away a tear and then flapped her hands at them all. "Now, everyone sit and let me serve up the food. No, you can't help. Sit. Everyone, just sit."

Knowing his mom was serious and that Shelley Walker liked nothing more than to fuss over her brood and feed them, he tugged Tessa's hand and held out a chair for her.

They sat for almost three hours, eating, laughing, and talking. Tessa asked questions about the ranch and their lives. They asked things that wouldn't cause Tessa any stress.

His mom patted Tessa's hand. "I know you'll want to get back to your Midnight Lake, but we'd like to ask you to stay one more day so we can have a family Christmas tomorrow. I know it's a few days early but we'd love to share an early Christmas with you both."

Tessa gasped beside him and shook her head. "We don't have any gifts. We haven't had time to do any shopping."

Beau held up a hand. "Stop, before Mom goes into her *Christmas isn't about presents speech*. We're not ten and we don't need gifts. It'll just be fun to get together. Say yes before she begs."

Flynn's dad reached over and tugged on Tessa's hair. "It'll be fun, little Daisy. Or maybe that should be Poinsettia."

Tessa smiled and her eyes glittered with hope. They left soon afterward with promises to return in the early afternoon for dinner.

As they drove, Tessa worried her bottom lip. "It's too late to do shopping tonight. We'll have to go in the morning."

"You heard them. We don't need to bring anything."

The look she shot him was full of horror. "Are you serious? They're hosting a Christmas dinner for us with one afternoon notice. Of course we need to bring things."

Her big, worried eyes had Flynn pulling onto a quiet side street and parking the Jeep. "Breathe, Tessa. There aren't any expectations here. It's just my family. They want it to be fun, not stressful."

He reached over and ran his thumb over the lip she kept gnawing on. Stress radiated off her in waves. "What's going on? What are you thinking?"

She blinked those luminous eyes a few times. "I don't know how to buy proper gifts. We didn't exchange gifts when I was a kid. I've never bought Christmas presents. I don't know what to do."

Flynn tried to keep the shock off his face. No gifts exchanged as a kid. No Christmas memories. With the chaotic frenzy of the Walker family in action, his Christmas memories were full of love and laughter. He might not remember all the gifts, but it was the feeling of family he remembered best.

He wanted her to have that, and she wouldn't have that if stress got in the way. "Okay. We'll figure it out. The best gifts make people smile. Any kind of smile, from silly to sappy. I think we should focus on silly for this year. What do you think?"

Her smile made him feel better than any trophy he'd received from his rodeo days. Now to spend time thinking of gifts rather than of making love to this woman.

Sounded like an evening of multi-tasking of the very best kind.

Tessa grinned as Beau and Morgan trash-talked while battling with their *Rock 'Em Sock 'Em* robots on the coffee table. She and Flynn had spent the morning at the thrift store and the grocery store. They'd laughed their way through learning to make brownies and wrapping gifts.

At the thrift store, they'd bought silly toys for everyone and board games for the afternoon. Clue, dominoes, Scrabble, Hungry Hippos, and Mastermind. They were all new to her and his entire family had cheered when she'd been the first to figure out *Who done it?* on the second game.

This is what she'd always wanted growing up. Love spilled from the Walkers like water from a fountain. Freely.

When Flynn and Shelley took over the robots, Marty offered to make a batch of hot chocolate for everyone. It was seventy degrees in Texas, but apparently it was a Christmas tradition. And the Walkers were all about traditions.

Tessa rose and smiled at Marty. "I'll give you a hand."

When they were in the kitchen, Marty moved to put a sauce pot on the stove. She frowned at it. "You're not using a kettle?"

Marty laughed. "For Christmas hot chocolate? I wouldn't dare. They'd throw me to the coyotes out there."

"How else do you make it?"

"Watch and learn, Little Bluebonnet."

She watched as he pulled out milk, cream, cocoa, and vanilla. "I've never seen anyone make hot chocolate from scratch before."

His wise eyes turned to her. "I think there are a lot of good things you haven't seen before." Sadness and kindness showed in his eyes, and she nodded because words were impossible.

Marty smiled softly and motioned her to come over to the stove where he taught her how to blend the ingredients. "It smells like Willy Wonka's factory in here."

"When did you see that movie?"

She smiled. "In the hospital when I was recovering."

"When you were getting stronger and learning to become a new version of yourself."

She nodded and Marty handed her the whisk. "Keep stirring." Then he used a huge knife to crush a candy cane. From the fridge, he brought out some whipped cream and chocolate sauce.

While she stirred, Marty leaned back against the counter and crossed his arms over his chest. Much as she'd seen his son do. Another kind of family tradition being passed down. She wondered if any of her mannerisms belonged to her mama.

Marty's serious voice broke into her thoughts. "My boy changed after that day you were here, you know."

Tessa's hand flinched but she kept stirring. Did she want to hear this?

"He became more."

That had her pausing to stare at him. "More?"

He motioned her to keep stirring. "More. More serious about his studies and his future. More interested in life outside the rodeo ring. More of a man than a boy."

When Marty grinned, the similarity between father and son was more pronounced. This was how Flynn would look and be in another twenty years. Strong. Steady. Thoughtful. It was a very good look.

Marty kept talking. "He wanted to be someone worthy of you."

"Of me?" Her voice squeaked and had Marty laughing.

"That was the day I saw my first boy fall in love."

Tessa's heart shivered.

"The day he thought you'd died was the worst day of his life and I hope he never has to go through anything like that again."

"I'm sorry."

Marty reached over and turned off the stove, motioned to her to put the pot on a cool element. Then he put his hands on her shoulders and waited until she looked up.

"Nothing to be sorry about. Nothing at all. I'm telling you to let you know his feelings aren't new or temporary. Finding you alive after all these years was the best thing that could have happened to him. I see the love he feels, see the joy in him. It's good. I wanted you to know that you became a part of our family on that day back in high school. And if my son's as smart as I think he is, it won't be long before he tries to make it official."

Tessa's mouth dropped open but nothing came out.

Marty kept talking. "You're not alone anymore, Tessa Flores. You're one of us and we couldn't be happier. Anything you need, anytime, all you need to do is ask."

Tears welled and her throat tightened.

Like Flynn, tears didn't seem to scare him. He laughed and pulled her in for a quick hug. "Now, let's make these hot chocolates special. How do you feel about adding a shot of Bailey's?"

CHAPTER 25
Second Chance

Back at Midnight Lake on Christmas morning, Tessa woke slowly, reluctant to leave the sexy dream she was having.

"There she is. Merry Christmas, Tessa."

She opened her eyes to find Flynn smiling down at her. His hand was between her legs and her body was lax and heavy with desire. Not a dream at all. "Merry Christmas."

Her words trailed off as Flynn changed the pace of his fingers and leaned down to kiss her. "We need to make sure our first Christmas together gets off to a good start."

She managed a laugh. "It's looking good from here."

He kissed her again and the then shifted his body until his shoulders pushed her legs apart. He grinned. "Looking good from here, too."

He proceeded to shatter her in the best way possible with his tongue. As the waves of pleasure were subsiding, he slid on a condom and slipped inside her, building her back up again.

When she was close, she reached up to cup his jaw. "With me, Flynn. Come with me."

"Always."

A long while—and a steamy shower—later, they opened the door to head downstairs. Ginger yowled from where she'd been dozing in the hallway.

Flynn scooped up the cat. "Did we lock you out? Sorry about that."

The cat snuggled into him as they negotiated the stairs and moved to the main room. Everyone looked up as they entered. "Finally. Don't you know it's Christmas morning?"

Tessa's face flushed but Flynn laughed. "We sure do."

Sam walked in carrying a tray filled with French toast and pancakes. "You almost missed breakfast. Go grab something from the kitchen."

Soon, the eleven of them were sitting around the table. Tansy and Sam. Aisling and Graham. Bella and Mitch. Joe, Josie, and Nico. And the two of them. Her new family. Her new home.

Her eyes misted with tears as she looked around the group. Across the table, Graham pointed his finger at her. "Nope. No tears, no sappy moments. This is our first Christmas together as a group and we're not spending it bawling."

She laughed along with everyone else and swallowed her tears. Sam picked up his mug. "For many of us, it's been a hell of a year. But we're stronger because of it. We've come through the other side of this year together. And I can't think of any people I'd rather spend it with. Merry Christmas, everyone."

They all lifted their mugs and cheered.

Once the food was eaten and cleared, they put Pennyworth on cleanup and gathered around the gorgeous live-edge table again. Aisling had built it and Tessa didn't know if she'd ever seen a more beautiful piece of furniture.

When Josie, Joe, and Nico had agreed to stay for Christmas, they'd all drawn names for a Secret Santa gift. Tessa had been relieved when she'd drawn Tansy's name. Tessa didn't have many creative aspects to her personality, but she understood Tansy's analytical brain.

Graham tossed a twelve-sided die from hand to hand. "Okay, number off. Whatever number I land on will give their gift. Whoever receives that gift will give theirs next."

They numbered off around the table and Graham tossed the die. "Who is eight?"

Tessa smiled. "That's me." She picked up her phone and sent the message she'd prepared. From somewhere outside the room, a phone beeped.

Sam rolled his eyes. "That's yours, Tans. Where'd you leave it?"

She laughed. "I have no idea."

Perfect.

While some of them protested that the phone call could wait, Tessa pressed another pre-made message and Sam's phone beeped. When he looked at the text, he grinned at Tessa.

Sam showed the phone to Tansy. "It's for you."

"What?"

Sam held up the phone for everyone to see. "It's a Tansy phone magnet."

Tansy grinned at her. "You made me a program?"

Tessa nodded. "It can be an app, but I thought this would be more fun."

Sam handed Tansy the phone and pressed the link Tessa had sent.

A voice came from the phone. *Eight meters north-west.*

Everyone laughed as Tansy moved across the room and into the hall. Every time she pressed the link, the voice updated the location.

Tansy returned moments later with her phone. "It even acts like a compass and points me in the direction. This is amazing, Tessa."

Tansy came around and hugged her. Sam followed suit. "I think this gift is as much for me as Tansy. Thanks."

"You can program it to find other things as well. All you need is a locator on the object."

As the gift-giving moved on, Flynn kissed her head. "That was perfect."

The gifts ranged from silly to serious. When it got to Sam, he grinned and stood up. "Mine's for you, Walker."

He walked around the table and dropped a worn silver star on the table in front of Flynn. Flynn's eyes widened and he picked it up reverently.

"We think it's an old deputy's star. Tansy found it in the basement one day in a bucket with a bunch of other stuff she won't let me throw away. Got someone to make it into one of those belt buckles you like."

The words Midnight Security had been etched into the star and

Flynn's eyes were a little glossy when he turned it over and over. "This is amazing, Sam. Thank you."

Flynn was next up and he'd picked Josie's name. He passed her a small notebook. "I'm not sure if you like to cook or not, but these are my mom's family recipes. Some of my dad's family too. A bunch of family members got together one day and collected all the handwritten recipes they could find. Mom compiled them and got them made up into a book. She printed off a dozen for each of us."

Josie's eyes glittered. "This is fabulous. I don't have any family recipes of my own, so I'm going to treasure this. Thank you."

Tessa didn't know Josie's story, but it was easy to see that Flynn had chosen exactly right.

Josie smiled. "And that leaves me with the final gift. For you, Tessa. Although it's a little bit for Flynn as well."

She handed over a beautiful frame that looked to be as old as the house around them. Her words confirmed it. "I found the frame in the basement and Tansy's okay with me using it."

Tessa flipped over the frame and gasped. Inside was a charcoal sketch of her and Flynn. They were standing on the dock with the lake in the background. Flynn was tucking her hair behind her ear and she was holding Ginger.

The sketch captured the love she felt in her heart and for a long moment she couldn't even find the words. "This is amazing Josie. It couldn't be more perfect. I love it. Thank you."

Then she hugged her new friend and wished she could do something to take away the pain she'd seen in her eyes.

Graham stood up. "Enough of the sappy stuff. Great job on the gifts everyone. Now, we got a fresh snowfall last night. Snowman building contest on now. Work in teams. Go."

Much later, Flynn squeezed Tessa's hand at the bottom of the stairs. "It's been a long day. May I offer you a lift?"

"It's been a wonderful day. Maybe the best day ever."

Her smile was full of wonder and delight. After the gift exchange, they'd made snowmen, had a snowball fight that included the dogs, and gone snowshoeing. After another family meal full of laughter and fun, they'd sung Christmas carols karaoke style and shared Christmas memories while the evening moved along.

Tessa's legs had to be worn out from the activities. They'd spaced everything out and she hadn't backed down at all, but he knew she had to be exhausted. He wanted to take care of her.

He waited and when Tessa nodded, he scooped her up and moved up the stairs to their room. The cat followed and once she was safely inside; he kicked the door closed and moved to the bathroom.

He set Tessa on the closed toilet seat and then started the water in the tub. She reached for the cabinet where she kept her bath stuff, but he beat her to it. "Try this one."

"What's this?"

"Gift number one. Bella helped. Something Christmassy she said."

Tessa grinned and tossed it in. Cinnamon and chocolate scents went along with the cookie-like design of the sphere. While the tub filled, he kissed her softly. "I'm going to grab you a glass of wine and let you relax for a bit."

"You could join me."

He grinned at her and kissed her. "I could, but I'm betting your legs would appreciate a chance to simply relax and soak up the heat. I'll be back."

When he returned, Tessa was leaned back against the back of the tub, eyes closed and music playing softly from her phone. He put the wine within reach and moved back to the other room.

With a grin, Flynn fluffed up the pillows and set the tray he'd brought up at the end of the bed. They'd agreed to extend the rules of the group exchange to their own personal gifts. Next year, they'd have more time, but with the month they'd survived, the gifts themselves would mean less than the simple act of being together.

When he heard the tub draining, he moved back into the room to find Tessa pushing to her feet, bubbles drifting down her body. His own reacted with lightning speed. "You're so damn beautiful, Tessa. Here, let me help."

She looked up and laughed. "What I am is awkward and slippery. I should have grabbed a towel first."

He grabbed one and wrapped it around her where she stood in the tub. He kissed her while he started to dry her off, then he lifted her out of the tub and finished the job.

When she was dry, he slipped one of his t-shirts over her head, making her smile. "I've never worn a boyfriend's shirt before."

She'd missed so damn much.

Tessa reached up and caressed his jaw. "That wasn't meant to make you sad. I'm not. I'm the happiest I've ever been. And I'm wearing my sexy boyfriend's shirt."

He held her hands out to the side and checked her over. "I like it. Especially the fact you're wearing nothing but skin underneath it. You keep checking off the fantasies I started way back when we were kids."

"Fantasies. I like the sound of that. Tell me more."

Laughing, he lifted her again and pulled her in for a kiss. "This is another."

He walked through and dropped her onto the bed and sat beside her. "Another one."

His hand slipped under the tee and up to her breast. "Another. And this is on the highlight reel."

Before he got carried away, he pulled away. "I'll show you a few more later, but I want to give you this first."

Suddenly nervous, he handed her the book. "This is the same book I gave Josie. It's from my folks too."

Tessa flipped it open and found his mom's inscription. *Welcome to the family, Tessa. Love Shelley and Marty.*

Tessa gasped softly and tears glistened through the huge smile as she beamed at him. "It's perfect. Thank you."

He rose to grab her phone from the bathroom, then handed it to her. "The second half, I'm going to drop to your phone."

Once she had hers, he dropped the folder and watched her tap it.

This gasp was softer and shakier. "Oh, Flynn. They're from that day. I've relived it so often in my memory, but I never thought I'd have photographs."

He shifted to tuck her into his side as she scrolled through the photos. He'd gathered all the ones everyone in his family had taken and compiled them in the folder.

He laughed when she pointed at the one of him standing on the railing of the corral, smiling down at her. "I was trying so hard to impress you that day. My brothers took a lot of pics so they could rag on me later."

Tessa with his mom in the garden. Making lunch. His dad showing her how to feed a horse. And so many of him and Tessa. On horseback. Grooming the horses. Eating. Laughing.

Wiping away tears, Tessa flipped between the photos again and again as they laughed and shared their memories. Eventually, she shifted so she could kiss him. "I love you, Flynn. That was the most perfect gift ever."

He lifted her onto his lap. "I love you too, Tessa."

His hands moved under her shirt again, but she pulled back with a smile. "My turn."

"Good. I definitely want to hear your fantasies."

With another laugh, she shifted enough to pull her phone up between them. "It appears we're all about using our phones for gifts this year. I'll drop yours."

A folder popped onto his phone and he opened it. "A family tree." He knew he was grinning like he had when he got his own saddle.

"I know how important your family is to you, and I thought you'd like to know who came before and what jobs they held."

He enlarged the screen to follow one of the branches.

Tessa pointed at one block. "You'll be able to see it better on a larger screen. The ones marked in green are connected to ranching and horses. You come by your rodeo skills honestly."

He zoomed back out to see green scattered all over the tree. "Very cool. What about the blue blocks?"

"Law enforcement."

"Seriously?" He hadn't known any of his ancestors were in law enforcement.

She nodded and pointed. "A Texas Ranger, a few sheriffs, and even one of the first female US Marshals way back in the 1890s."

"That's amazing."

Tessa tapped the block and it brought up a pop-up, giving Flynn a grainy photo and brief biography of the woman. He clicked around several of the blocks, skimming snippets of Walker family history.

Then he put down the phone and cupped Tessa's face. "It's perfect, absolutely perfect. Thank you. But enough about history. I'd like to focus on the present for a little while."

Tessa giggled. "That was a present."

He rolled his eyes as he laughed with her. "I'm thinking more about this kind of present."

And then he kissed her because she was his present.

And his future.

Ten weeks later

Tessa was glad she'd worn gloves. It might be spring, but Vermont hadn't read the memo. The ice was breaking up over Midnight Lake and Tessa wanted to collect data on her turtles. She'd worried about them over the winter, which had been colder than average.

"Looks like we're coming up on your first location." Flynn said from the back of the canoe. "Hang on."

He back paddled and then used the paddle to keep them in place. "Do your magic."

She laughed. "It's hardly magic."

"Not yet. But with the data you collect, you always create magic."

He said the most amazing things. And she'd learned he was always serious when he said them. He believed in her. The months since Christmas had brought them closer and more in love than ever before. What else would bring the man out in a canoe when the wind chill had temperatures hovering around twenty?

She checked the app to get as close to the original location as possible and used her stick to take measurements. She input the distance to the first point of resistance, then reached further to find a hard substance. Her turtle. "He's still there."

"I'm glad I'm not a turtle. That's a hell of a way to spend the winter."

For the next few hours, they drifted along the lake. In almost all of her locations, she found what she assumed were turtles. The few spots she didn't find anything, she hoped the turtles had moved on after she'd taken the measurements.

Finally, they reached the far end of the lake and Flynn steered them toward the dock of the cabin where they'd first talked all those months ago. "Been a while since we were here."

Tessa nodded, memories flooding her. She'd been terrified that day, even more terrified than when she'd woken up from her coma. He'd been so angry. A few months later and she was happier than she'd ever been.

Flynn popped up to the dock and she handed him the ropes to tie the canoe. Then he lifted her easily. All those months ago, it had been embarrassing for him to see her weakness. Now, it didn't bother her at all. He knew everything about her, knew the reasons for her scars. And he loved her anyway.

Inside the cabin, she fired up the pellet stove. The cabin blocked the wind, but it was still cold inside. Flynn grabbed the quilt off the bed and moved to wrap it around her. "You're freezing."

That made her laugh. "So are you. Thanks for counting turtles with me. You didn't have to do that."

He grinned. "As a kid, I never imagined paddling a canoe while there was snow on the ground and searching the bottom of a lake for snoozing turtles."

"Me neither."

He hugged her and swayed them slightly back and forth. "Ever think about going back to school and getting the qualifications to teach math like you always wanted? You're free to do that now."

She opened her mouth to respond, but realized she didn't have a ready answer. "I honestly haven't thought about it."

He kissed her nose. "Think about it. You've got choices now. You need to do what makes you happy."

She did have choices. In large part to the man holding her closely. She shifted the thoughts about in her head. What did she want?

And that answer cleared it all up for her.

Tessa used a finger to lightly poke Flynn's chest and he backed up a step. Then another. She moved with him, kept her other arm around him.

"What are you doing?"

She grinned at the confusion on his face. "I'm doing what makes me happy." Then she poked him again. Her cowboy went willingly and when his legs backed into the bed, he grinned.

With a final poke, he tumbled back to the bed, with her in his arms.

She rubbed the spot she'd poked then kissed it. "Remember the last time we were here?"

Flynn nodded and sighed. "Everything was such a mess back then. I was so angry."

"You had a right to be."

He rolled them over and then took his weight on his elbows. "No. I didn't."

She smiled. "Your world had been turned upside down. Everything you'd thought about me for the past decade was proven wrong. You were entitled to a hissy fit or two."

Flynn's eyes widened. "Hissy fit? I don't have hissy fits."

Tessa laughed. "If you say so. You were entitled to storm off in a manly fashion."

He nodded, eyes twinkling. "Much better. Although I think there might have been a bit of cowboy swagger in there."

"Sexy cowboy swagger." She ran her fingers along his scruffy jaw. "You know what I was thinking then?"

"You were thinking of disappearing on me."

She nodded. "Aside from that. I was thinking that I wanted to stay right here in this bed with you forever. I wanted to forget the past, forget the threats, forget the fear. I wanted to strip you naked and lick you from top to bottom. I wanted you to hold me and make love to me. Forever."

Flynn's eyes had misted as she spoke. "I wanted all that, too. Even through the anger and the confusion and the fear. I wanted that future with you from the first moment."

"And now we have it. Our second chance."

He kissed her, long and deep. Emotions swirled inside her and each one was positive and happy.

"I don't want to go back to school. I don't want to teach Math anymore. Instead, I want to stay right here at Midnight Lake and count turtles and birds and frogs. I want to figure out how we can learn from them to help cope with climate change, and how we can stop screwing up the earth. I want to watch you and the others make the world a safer place as Tansy figures out how to make everything better. I want Midnight Lake and I want you."

"Sounds like one hell of a plan." Then he kissed her again with enough intensity, she wondered that her body didn't start to glow.

When they broke apart to breathe, he grinned. "I'm never going to get enough of you. You're stuck with me."

She laughed. "No place I'd rather be."

Bonus Scene (Christmas Day): Nico
Late on Christmas, Nico leaned against the railing on the deck and watched the night. Midnight Lake was peaceful and quiet. It was a good place. A place of hope and possibilities.

His friends were making it their home.

Tansy and Sam had started something amazing. A mix of science and safety. A place to learn and to teach.

Everyone who'd joined in had brought something special with them. And found something special at the same time.

Graham and Aisling had worked through their past. Graham was an integral part of Midnight Security and Aisling was doing amazing things with the old lodge. Mitch and Bella were starting a new firehall in town. Now his buddy Flynn had found the girl he'd thought was dead. And they'd found their peace and their future.

In some ways, Midnight Lake reminded him of the home he'd grown up in. His folks had created a place that was also full of peace and possibilities. How many kids had they fostered? Kids who'd arrived scared and wary.

Every single one of those kids had learned that there *were* safe places in the world. Havens where people actually gave a shit. Places they could be safe, filled with people they could trust.

All those kids had learned that the world truly was filled with possibilities, not just fear and anger.

His parents loved what his buddies were creating here at Midnight Lake. They just wished it was closer to Sacramento. When he'd video chatted with them earlier, they'd planned a visit for later in January. They would never leave their foster kids for Christmas because many of those kids had never experienced the wonders that came with this time of year. The Rivera house dripped Christmas and love from every corner. His folks made sure their kids always had at least one Christmas memory they could treasure. Nico would fly out in the morning to see them for a few days.

Could he do peaceful full time? Sam was pestering both him and Joe to put down roots here. Nico didn't know if he could do it. He wasn't sure he was made for this kind of life.

He turned to lean back on the railing and study the lodge.

Windows were dark in most of the rooms. A low light shone through a window on the third floor. As he counted, he realized it was the room Josie had chosen.

She'd dropped everything in her life to come north with them to help out, without knowing Tessa at all. She'd initially given Nico a hard time about coming, but then she'd not only come, but she'd added on a couple of days to celebrate Christmas with them.

Where was her family? Why wasn't she with them? Nico didn't have much trouble reading people, but Josie Ellis was a puzzle. Brash and bold. Dressed like a sexy hippie half the time. What was her story?

Not that he needed to know. It was simply a byproduct of being a profiler. He wanted to know everyone's story.

The ring of his phone surprised him. Roman Delgado's name showed on the screen and Nico's heart sank. "Roman."

His partner's voice was grim when he spoke. "He's killed another one."

Nico turned his back on the peace of the lodge. "Where?"

"Vegas."

"You're sure?" Which was a stupid question because Roman

wouldn't have called if he wasn't sure. "Sorry. You're sure. She fits the type?"

"To every sexy curve and each long black curl. They're holding the scene for us."

"I'll be there as soon as I can. Text me the info."

He shoved off the railing and moved to pack. Christmas break was over.

Thank you!

Thank you for reading! If you enjoyed the story, please consider leaving a review at any (or all!) of your favourite retailers.

To find out more about Jemi, please check out her website at jemifraser.com. There, you can sign up for her newsletter and bonus scenes featuring your favourite characters.

Jemi Fraser writes romantic suspense filled with hope, heart, and humour. Her stories combine her love of mystery with the satisfaction of a Happy Ever After.

Armed with a mug of tea and freshly-baked cookies, Jemi is living out her own HEA in beautiful Northern Ontario.

Also by Jemi Fraser

Small Town Heroes Romantic Suspense Series

Built Of Secrets (Book 1)

Built Of Strength (Book 2)

Built Of Flames (Book 3)

Built Of Second Chances (Book 4)

Built Of Illusions (Book 5)

Built Of Steel (Book 6)

Bloo Moose Romantic Suspense Series

Reaching For Normal (Book 1)

Reaching For Risks (Book 2)

Reaching For Everything (Book 3)

Reaching For Balance (Book 4)

Reaching For Christmas (Book 5)

Reaching For Trust (Book 6)

Reaching For Roots (Book 7)

Reaching For Family (Book 8)

Reaching For Home (Book 9)

Reaching For More (Book 10)

Bloo Moose Box Sets

Bloo Moose Box Set 1 (Books 1-3)

Bloo Moose Box Set #2 (Books 4-6)

Bloo Moose Box Set #3 (Books 7-9)

Acknowledgments

A huge thank you to Carol for all the brilliant advice throughout the building of this book. Thanks as well to Pamela and Renée. You're always ready with early eyes for these stories. Your support means everything!

Thanks as always to my cover creator JB. I love how you've brought the Small Town Heroes to life with your visions.

The online writing community is a wonderful place. There are so many supportive people who are willing to help each other. Cheers to everyone who reaches back and those who reach forward!

And, of course, a huge thank you to the readers who take a chance on a new author and a new series. Every reader, every review, every kind word means more than you'll ever know!

Ingram Content Group UK Ltd.
Milton Keynes UK
UKHW010824270623
424112UK00001B/86

9 798223 036647